GO GENTLY,
GAIJIN

By the same author

GO GENTLY, GAIJIN

James Melville

St. Martin's Press
New York

Library of Congress Cataloging in Publication Data

Melville, James.
    Go gently, gaijin.

    I. Title.
PR6063.E439G6   1986   823'.914   86-13033
ISBN 0-312-32989-X

First published in Great Britain by Martin Secker & Warburg Limited.

First U. S. Edition

10 9 8 7 6 5 4 3 2 1

亜捻昆亜人
殺人事件

AUTHOR'S NOTE

So far as I am aware, there is no such organisation as the Kinki International Students' Society (KISS). There may well be groups with names and objectives which bear some resemblance to those I have attributed to my imaginary society, though. Moreover, Hyogo is a real prefecture, and its police force is based in the city of Kobe, where there is a sizeable Islamic community whose religious life is centred on a mosque in the location I describe. The Takarazuka All-Girl Revue Company is one of the most famous entertainment organisations in Japan, its home theatre being in the town of that name situated not far from the hot-spring resort of Arima and Kobe itself. It is therefore, perhaps more than usually important for me to assure readers that all the characters in this story are entirely fictional and bear no relation to any living person.

GO GENTLY, GAIJIN

Chapter I

"It's just along here, not far," Junko Migishima said to her husband Ken'ichi as they rounded the corner near the American Pharmacy and turned into a narrower street leading off the popular shopping thoroughfare of Tor Road in Kobe. It was a beautiful April day, and though the hills above the city are not particularly well supplied with flowering cherries, smudges of the palest pink could be seen here and there in the distance against the young green of the woodland. In the previous week or two the Japanese newspapers had been lamenting the late arrival of spring, and the charts displayed every night on television during the weather report showing the slow advance of the "cherry-blossom front" from the south of the country had been the subject of much sucking of teeth from the male weatherpersons and of brave, encouraging words from the girls.

At last all was well, though, and the Migishimas could not have had more agreeable weather for one of their rare and therefore precious days off together. Although two or three

1

years of close association with the trendy Inspector Jiro Kimura had had their effect on Migishima's appearance, he still bore many of the conventional outward marks of the policeman. His burly frame had a comfortable solidity to it, giving his walk a stateliness which made him look rather more than his twenty-eight years, and though under pressure from Kimura he had smartened up his wardrobe, it would not have taken a Sherlock Holmes to decide that here might well be a member of the Hyogo prefectural police force in plain clothes. The fact that Junko Migishima also served in that force and was one of the brightest stars of its criminal investigation section was much better disguised.

Junko was twenty-five, and had not the smallest intention of assuming the normal subdued protective colouring of most young married Japanese women. Her legs were better than average and she had welcomed the return of short skirts, not to mention the milder weather. That day she was showing quite a lot of the legs in question under a white denim skirt worn with a baggy cherry-red sweatshirt, and swung along jauntily at her large husband's side in the bright sunshine, quite enjoying the occasional admiring glances she received from passers-by including some of Kobe's sizeable community of Westerners for whom bustling Tor Road is the effective centre of the city. It was lunchtime, but after an hour's window-shopping in the covered Motomachi arcades the Migishimas had decided to stroll in the sunshine and wait until after the noon rush to find something to eat.

"Did Inspector Hara suggest that you should have a look at the mosque, then?" Although his own boss Kimura had soon begun to refer to his recently appointed colleague the head of the criminal investigation section by a variety of dismissive nicknames, of which "The Professor" was becoming his favourite, Migishima was a stickler for the proprieties.

"What an idea!" Junko grinned up at him and gave him a little punch in the side. She was highly amused. "Quite the reverse. He explained at least four times to me that women aren't allowed into mosques and that, Islamic ways being

2

what they are, there's obviously no point in my trying to interview anyone except the girl herself. He's got a pile of books about Islam on his desk and keeps on about their attitudes to women and the family."

Migishima paused, gazing in some puzzlement at the façade of an establishment announcing itself in English to be a Dogs' Hospital. "It's on the other side of the road," Junko pointed out, and turned him gently round, after which she allowed him to pilot her across. When they reached the other side they stood together and looked at a faded notice behind dirty glass in a frame fixed to the railings. Alongside a notice hand-written in Arabic was a simple announcement typed in English:

FRIDAY PRAYERS 12.30

Though terse, it was intelligible to both of them, and Migishima bent to peer at the foot of the yellowing sheet. "It says here that the Imam is called Huseyim Ibn Alim Kilki, but – oh, this is ridiculous, the notice is dated 1975! You'd think they'd have put up a new one within ten years, wouldn't you?"

As Junko scrutinised the notice in her turn Migishima straightened up and spoke in a consciously fair-minded way. "The situation's inevitably complicated. There's no denying that Inspector Hara *is* in charge of criminal investigation. All the same, Inspector Kimura obviously knows more about the foreign community in Kobe. It's our job to keep an eye on them, after all," he added, modestly. "So our two sections will have to work together."

Junko looked up at him sideways, her urchin face alive with mischief. "They will, won't they?" she said, her mobile mouth revealing her continuing amusement in reflecting on the developing relationship between the scholarly, earnest Inspector Takeshi Hara and the conceited, often insufferably cocky Inspector Kimura of the curiously named Foreign Affairs Section, with his fluent English, serviceable French, fashionable imported clothes and frequent monumental blunders.

"We arrived just at the right time," Junko then said contentedly. "They must be in the middle of their Friday prayers now: it's five to one. I wonder how many people there are in there?" It was difficult from the road to estimate the size of the stucco building with its small forecourt behind the railings.

"So far as we've been told, they get about fifty or sixty men coming here most weeks," Migishima said, "but that's not surprising. There are some hundreds of Moslems living in the Kobe area, after all."

"Really? *Hundreds?* Where do they all come from?" Junko was genuinely surprised.

"Well, the only Islamic consular people here are the Indonesians. I suppose there may be one or two among the Indians, too. But a lot of the foreigners who work in Osaka actually live in the Kobe area, of course. It's mostly the business community where you find the Moslems, Pakistanis, Bangladeshis, Malaysians, Indonesians, a few Arabs. They're more or less permanent, but then on top of them you have seamen from merchant ships, and foreign students. Hardly ever any tourists, needless to say."

"There aren't more than a handful of students, either," Junko said as they both peered through the railings. The main doors of the mosque were ajar and she thought she could hear a thin voice chanting, interspersed with the rumble of occasional responses, but the noise of the traffic effectively drowned the sound. "I looked through the Kobe University Bulletin out of curiosity and they only have a couple of Indonesians, a few Malaysians and, oh, two Iranians. They're Islamic too, aren't they?"

"They certainly are. But don't forget the other universities in the area. We have records of at least five times that number of students from Islamic countries. Look, they seem to be coming out."

Men were beginning to straggle out of the mosque and Junko looked at them with open interest: it was rare even in

4

Kobe to see foreigners together in any numbers, and these constituted an interestingly mixed bag. The first out was a white-haired, stocky old man in shabby cotton trousers and a pin-striped jacket belonging to a cheap suit. He was followed by a younger, thickset man with a much darker skin and a mop of black hair who was wearing a gaudily multicoloured shirt cut to fit tightly round his midriff, with an exaggeratedly wide open collar. His pale, almost creamy brown trousers were an equally snug fit around his hips and buttocks but flared out at the bottoms, which almost swept the ground. He was in conversation with a thin-faced middle-aged man in a smart dark suit, and they paused outside the gate before parting. Then, as the Migishimas watched, the older of the two crossed the road to an open-fronted shop selling cigarettes and chocolate.

"They aren't supposed to drink alcohol, you know," Junko whispered knowingly. "But they smoke a lot. Ooh, look, there's a *haji*. He's been to Mecca." She discreetly indicated a wispy, dessicated-looking man who had just come out of the mosque. "You can tell by his white cap. Inspector Hara explained it to me." Two young men in jeans and T-shirts emerged after that. They looked like students and were clearly in a hurry, pushing rather rudely through the other people in the doorway and turning right out of the gate, striding quickly together away from the Tor Road direction.

"They must have a lecture to go to," Migishima said indulgently. "That tall one on the left certainly had enough books under his arm." He turned back to look at the men now streaming out of the mosque, some of them stooping in the sunshine to tie shoelaces, while others paused to exchange a few words, but lost interest rapidly as he became more and more aware of the pangs of hunger. After another minute he touched Junko's arm, and was about to suggest that they should move on when he realised that some kind of disturbance seemed to be taking place near the entrance to the mosque and that those of the men lingering outside who were nearest to the tall double doors had turned to look back.

5

Then a man in a dark suit pushed his way through them and made for the gate. He looked both distressed and angry as he rushed pass the Migishimas and made off in the same direction as most of the other departing worshippers. He didn't get far. In fact he was about ten yards from the junction with Tor Road when a taxi roared past the mosque, struck the man obliquely and flung him against a concrete electricity-supply pole before squealing round the corner and disappearing. What followed was like a slow motion sequence in a film as the Migishimas gaped in horror. It was as though the man embraced the pole for a second or two before sliding gently to the ground like a cartoon drunk: but then they saw the blood and caught a sickening glimpse of what had been his face.

Junko pulled herself together first. "Run!" she shrieked at her husband. "That taxi!" Then she darted across the narrow street to a small open-fronted chemist's shop outside which was one of the ubiquitous red pay telephones, picked up the receiver and dialled 110 for an ambulance. By the time she had finished a small crowd had assembled, among them the man who had earlier crossed the road to buy cigarettes. A man in a white coat from the chemist's was on his knees beside the still, huddled figure on the roadside, and a uniformed policeman was approaching at a run, followed Migishima.

There was nothing anybody could do for the victim who must have died almost instantly, and Migishima had been too late to spot the taxi in crowded Tor Road. After an ambulance had arrived and left again with its bloody burden the traffic police set to work to photograph skid marks and measure distances to the pathetic chalk outline on the bloodstained road, officiously busy with their clip-boards and big wind-up tape measures. Junko and her husband tried to help by asking the onlookers if anyone could remember the taxi's registration number, but without success. The Migishimas were themselves questioned by the sergeant directing the proceedings, who was astounded to discover that they were both police officers and glanced frequently

6

with suspicion and incredulity at Junko in her abbreviated skirt.

After what seemed like a long time they were free to go and did in fact get as far as a nearby coffee shop where they sat over heavily sweetened cups of coffee and Migishima discovered that he was trembling. Junko herself was pale, but insistent that she didn't want to go home. On the contrary, she wanted to go back to look at the mosque again and five minutes later they were arguing with each other outside the now closed gates, their backs to the scene of the hit-and-run horror. "I'm *perfectly all right!*" Junko sounded exasperated. "And in any case there are some things I want to do, people I want to talk to around here. So calm down, and leave me to get on. Go and catch the bus to Arima: you mustn't be late for the party. I'll see you at home tonight."

Migishima was still hesitating indecisively when they both heard the sound of a siren approaching. A few seconds later a police car was driven at speed round the corner of the street and brought to a dramatic halt outside the gates. At the same time one of the double doors of the mosque opened and a fine-looking old gentleman with a beard and wearing flowing robes came out and stood in an attitude of immense dignity at the top of the stone steps.

The police driver jumped out and ran to open the rear door, and Inspector Takeshi Hara awkwardly extricated himself from the back seat and emerged, blinking; a pale, moon-faced man who unconsciously stooped, as many tall but diffident people do, but nevertheless towered over his driver and even the burly Migishima who drew himself up and stood stiffly to attention. Hara was narrow-shouldered but plump around the middle, and looked a little like General de Gaulle as he acknowledged their presence with a courteous nod.

Then a frown wrinkled his forehead and he fixed his attention on Junko. "I am surprised to find you here, Officer Migishima." He had a donnish, precise way of speaking, as though measuring out his words one by one.

"Off duty, sir," Junko said crisply. "Witnessed a fatal

7

accident. About an hour ago. A member of the congregation came out of the mosque and was hit by a taxi travelling at speed and flung against that electricity-supply pole. We've been assisting the traffic police."

"Indeed? A member of the congregation? My own appointment is with the Imam whom I observe at the door. Most unfortunate. I greatly fear that he will have been shocked and distressed by this occurrence." He suddenly pursed his lips and looked down at Junko with schoolmasterly displeasure. "I hope very much, officer, that you have not attempted to enter the mosque precincts. . ."

Inspector Hara's voice trailed away as he turned to her husband, removed his granny glasses, polished them carefully and then replaced them. "And you, officer. The victim was presumably a foreigner. I take it that you are not here under the instructions of Inspector Kimura?"

Migishima stiffened even more. "No, sir. I'm off duty too. Just leaving, sir." Although in plain clothes he saluted. "On my way to the Superintendent's celebration dinner at Arima, sir," he could not resist adding as he turned away, being rewarded with a wink and a momentary kissing movement of the lips from Junko.

Inspector Hara had been transferred from Nagasaki to the Hyogo headquarters staff in Kobe only within the past few weeks, and was therefore not involved in the festivities, but Junko had reported that he was less than happy about his exclusion. Migishima therefore rather enjoyed rubbing it in. All the same, he was sorry to have to leave Junko even though the dinner was to be a stag affair and they would have parted company anyway after another hour or so. It was the first time he had seen his wife in the company of Inspector Hara, and he was gratified by the realisation that she seemed not to be intimidated by her new boss in the least. The encounter was in fact timely. A hit-and-run case involving a fatality was a serious criminal matter, and Junko would in any case have had to report her presence at the scene at the earliest opportunity. Since it involved a foreigner, his own superior

8

Kimura would also have to be brought in, and would no doubt appreciate an early, informal briefing about the shocking episode during the course of the evening ahead.

Migishima therefore departed, looking back after a few moments to observe Inspector Hara mounting the steps to the dignitary he had identified as the Imam of the mosque, while his wife Junko waited with apparent equanimity outside the gates.

Chapter II

Happily ignorant of the flurry of activity at the mosque in Kobe, Superintendent Tetsuo Otani paused, bent and peered at the plaque affixed to the outside wall of the public bathhouse at the Arima Hot Spring resort, then took out his glasses, put them on and had a second look at the inscription. After that he straightened up and looked solemnly at his wife Hanae. "Just the thing," he remarked. "It says the waters of these springs have been renowned as being specially good for rheumatism, neurosis and female disorders ever since an Emperor first visited the place in 638 A.D. Are you sure you won't stay?"

Hanae smiled, as much to herself as to her husband, shaking her head as she did so. "No, thank you. I've had a lovely day, and the bus leaves for Sannomiya in twenty minutes. I shall be home within an hour or so. You know quite well you'll enjoy yourself much more if it's just you and the others. I know you won't be late, anyway."

Otani could not contradict her with any real conviction, but was nevertheless regretful as they strolled towards the bus-stop chatting in a desultory way..On an impulse he bought her a souvenir box of the locally-made speciality, "Arima Carbonicid Cakes". Then he made sure she had her five hundred yen bus fare ready to hand, saw her on board and bowed slightly in acknowledgement of Hanae's farewell wave as the bus moved off and disappeared round a bend in the road.

It had indeed been a very enjoyable day, and he hoped that the celebration dinner that his colleagues had arranged in his honour at the Arima Grand View Hotel to mark the tenth anniversary of his appointment to command the Hyogo force would not turn out to be something of an anticlimax. Hanae had been invited, and that gesture in itself was flatteringly out of the ordinary. She was duly touched, but never had the slightest intention of accepting and being the only woman guest among a boozy collection of off-duty police officers, thus spoiling their fun by inhibiting their ribald exchanges with the waitresses.

It had been a happy compromise for Otani to take a day's leave and for them both to go by bus up to Arima in the morning to spend a few hours wandering about the little town and its surroundings before he presented himself to his colleagues at the appointed hour of 5 p.m. and joined them in the hotel's communal hot-spring bath to relax in, and benefit from, the therapeutic properties of the red, mineral-rich waters before the banquet.

Arima Onsen is one of the oldest of the hundreds of hot-spring resorts in Japan, having been recognised and patronised as such since the seventh century when the Imperial capital was in the ancient city of Nara. Since then the scalding waters had never ceased to bubble out of the rocks not far from the summit of Mount Rokko, on the seaward foothills of which the Otanis lived in the old wooden house he had been brought up in as a boy in the thirties. In those days it had been quite an adventure to visit Arima: now it was a mere half-an-hour away by car, or forty minutes on the hourly bus from nearby Kobe. There was also a train service, and even a cable

11

car for the more adventurous.

Even so, it had been something like fifteen years since the Otanis had bothered to visit the place, and they had at first been disappointed when the brief prospect of small fields and woodland which came into view as their bus emerged from the new 7-kilometre Kobe Tunnel soon gave way to a rash of dormitory housing development which extended virtually all the way to the approach road to Arima proper. The town itself had changed a lot, too. Hot-spring resorts in Japan are generally characterised by an atmosphere of cheery vulgarity, and the tourist shops with their brightly coloured gimcrack souvenirs and soft-drink machines on every corner didn't bother Otani. It was the huge new-style hotels which had appeared since his last visit which upset him, and Hanae had found him glum and uncommunicative as they trudged up the long flight of stone steps to the old Buddhist temple above the town past just such an establishment, the Royal Hotel, which had been·built within the temple's very precincts.

Everything had suddenly become right again when they pressed on up the hillside, perspiring in the warm spring sunshine, and came to the even more ancient Shinto shrine, tranquil and unspoiled, and commanding a fine view of Arima cupped in wooded hills. Even the multi-storey hotels looked less oppressive rearing up out of the fresh green froth of young leaves far below, and the tiled roofs of a number of surviving old-fashioned inns comforted Otani's conservative eye. After a while they had gone on, up a steep woodland path to the so-called "Plum Woods Viewing Crest" of the Mount Otago Park, over fifteen hundred feet above sea-level. The air was soft and heavy with sunshine and the perfume of pine resin, and Hanae had not wanted to leave the quiet little open space which they had entirely to themselves at that hour on a weekday, and from where they could see the pretty little mountain known as the "Arima Fuji" because of its resemblance to its revered namesake, the Takahara Golf Club to the north, and other places of interest thoughtfully indicated on an outline map engraved on a metal plate set into a stone safety parapet equipped with coin-operated binoculars on a pedestal.

Otani had spoiled things momentarily by pointing out to Hanae that the body of a murder victim toppled over the parapet might lie undiscovered in the dense undergrowth a hundred feet and more below for years. A detective novel on this theme might, he thought, be entitled *Death Takes a Tumble* or something along those lines. While disapproving of this line of speculation, Hanae had welcomed the evidence it constituted of a return on Otani's part to his normal equable good humour, and they had made their way down to the town again very happily to enjoy a late lunch, at a simple traditional restaurant they found tucked away in a back street behind the Buddhist temple, and a leisurely stroll round the few shops in the narrow main street. They were both pleased to find some very old ones still in business, open-fronted but dark and cool inside, and Hanae was able to point out an ancient carved panel with gilded letters at the back of one of them which recorded the fact that a former proprietor, one Kuhai Yoda, had received an award for his bamboo ware at the Chicago Exhibition of 1893.

Otani was so taken with it that he went back for another look after seeing Hanae off, and enjoyed a nostalgic chat about the old days with the elderly lady presiding over an appetising and aromatic display of pickles in wooden tubs. At her insistence he sampled a few and bought some pungent lotus root to take back to Rokko with him at the end of the evening. Then it was time to head for the Grand View Hotel, a few minutes' walk away, if he was to arrive, with proper Japanese courtesy, five or ten minutes before the time specified and thus reassure his hosts that he was actually going to turn up.

The Grand View Hotel was very much in the modern style, its automatic glass doors partially obliterated by stickers indicating which credit cards were accepted and to which chains of hotels and travel bureaux it was affiliated. There was, however, no Rotary Club sign: Otani was a loyal if occasionally less than enthusiastic Rotarian and presumed that his Arima brethren must meet weekly in some other, even fancier hostelry. He turned his attention to the vertically ruled blackboard on an easel placed to one side of the main doors, listing in elegant white-painted calligraphy the names of the principal guests expected that day, and noted that somebody had done him proud. The first of the seven or eight announcements read as follows:

PEONY ROOM
Festive Banquet to Honour
The Respected Head
of the Hyogo Police Force
OTANI TETSUO

A rather good-looking woman in a pink kimono bowed very low in welcome as Otani entered the hotel. Although the lobby was carpeted, tradition was observed at least to the extent that guests removed their shoes and placed them in a rack before stepping up and into one of the array of pairs of backless slippers lined up in readiness. Otani identified himself as he did this, being treated to an even more ceremonious stream of honorifics in consequence. Then he was ushered to the lift and whisked to the third floor, along a carpeted corridor and into a kind of antechamber adjoining the Peony Room, where the first sight that met his startled eyes was that of a pair of voluminous underpants draping Inspector "Ninja" Noguchi's massive backside. His old friend and colleague was in the process of removing his trousers, and neither he nor Otani's escort showed the least embarrassment. Indeed the kimono-clad lady courteously assisted Noguchi into a blue and white cotton *yukata* as the two men greeted each other, and was obviously quite ready to stay and lend similar assistance to Otani. He politely declined, however, and she took her leave with many expressions of respect.

"Everybody here already, Ninja?" Otani enquired, looking at the piles of clothing which littered the tatami-matted

14

floor and beginning to take off his own clothes. He saw that there was but one neatly-folded yukata and folded *obi* sash left in a deep lacquer tray in one corner.

Noguchi nodded, securing his own sash in front and then twisting it round so that the bow fetched up slightly askew over one majestic buttock. "Just timed it right," he rumbled, and waited while Otani got into similar deshabille. Then Noguchi padded gravely across the tatami and slid open the *fusuma* screen which divided the antechamber from the main banqueting room. Otani entered to a roar of welcome from the three dozen or so men within, some of them standing about with cups of green tea in their hands, others sitting cross-legged on flat *zabuton* cushions smoking.

For a few moments as his hosts assumed a kneeling position and bowed low to their commander and Otani humbly returned their courtesy, and again half an hour or so later during the toast in *sake* which marked the commencement of the banquet, everything was gravity and formality; but the rest of the proceedings until almost eight-thirty were marked by increasingly uninhibited good humour. The sight of Noguchi wallowing in the huge bath with a dozen other police officers, his hand-towel balanced on his head, and being earnestly addressed by the grizzled head of the Traffic Section, whose glasses were completely fogged with steam, was something Otani made a mental note to describe to Hanae later. During the meal which was served immediately after the bath Otani had to clear his throat several times before he had his voice under enough control to respond to the incompetent but touching tribute paid to him by one of the divisional inspectors deputed to address the company on behalf of all non-headquarters officers under Otani's command.

He hardly noticed what he was eating as dish after dish was placed before him by one of the four kimono-clad waitresses who had their work cut out keeping beer and whisky glasses and *sake* cups replenished as well as serving the multi-course meal, and felt pleasantly fuddled and maudlin by the time he

15

was called upon to sing. The hotel people had provided a *karaoke* kit: a microphone and amplifier with backing tapes for amateur songsters, and Otani's sentimental rendition of one of the most popular songs of the time, with its frequent references to happiness, loneliness, pine trees and the sighing of bamboo leaves, brought the house down.

Even towards the end of the party Otani was however very far from drunk. Melon had been served by way of dessert, and the waitresses were pouring green tea as a sign that the festivities were coming to an end, even though some of the men there had arranged to stay overnight. Otani was actually glancing furtively at his watch and on the point of making a move to leave when he noticed the woman who had greeted him on arrival at the hotel enter the room unobtrusively and whisper to Patrolman Migishima, who, as the most junior member of the company, was nearest the door. Migishima felt flattered to be there at all, even though it was at the behest of his boss Kimura who had organised the celebrations and decided that he might need his services during the course of the evening.

Kimura himself was busy, flirting archly with one of the waitresses, and did not notice Migishima's embarrassed attempts to attract his attention until the young man went over to him and muttered directly into his ear. Then he hastily scrambled up and went with Migishima to the door where Otani saw him in brief but seemingly serious conversation with the woman before all three disappeared. Nobody else seemed to have noticed, so Otani murmured briefly to Noguchi, who, as the oldest officer present, was seated at his side, and Noguchi clapped his hands with electrifying effect, announcing as he did so that the guest of honour was about to leave.

Two or three sentences of thanks were enough, but Otani then had to press his colleagues to remain seated, explaining that he wished to leave very unobtrusively. Some of them looked slightly surprised, since convention really required that they should crowd to the front entrance to wave and bow

16

him away, but they had all drunk enough to do as they were bidden, and soon he and Noguchi were back in the ante-chamber and slipping quickly into their clothes while Otani told his most trusted associate what he had noticed. They were fully dressed except for their shoes and were able to leave with a cheery wave by the time the first of the other guests began stumbling in from the Peony Room in search of their clothes.

A young maid was standing indecisively in the corridor outside and one look at the expression on her face told Otani that she knew where Kimura and the others were. Otani spoke to her with grave and reassuring authority, and without a word she led them round the corner and up one flight of service stairs, then a short way along a similar corridor to the open doorway of a guest room, at which point she fled. There was no mistaking Kimura's voice from within, and Otani entered.

It was a good-sized room of eight mats, about twelve feet square not counting the wooden-floored area by the window which contained two armchairs and a coffee-table. A man's jacket and a pair of trousers were draped over the back of one of the chairs, and a shirt and other items of clothing had been tossed on to the seat. There was a pair of men's shoes on the floor beside the chair. Given the extra wooden-floored area there was plenty of space to move about in the main part of the room, even though bedding for two was laid out on the tatami. Moreover, the room was equipped with its own private bathroom, a miniaturised version of the men's and women's communal bathrooms below. Such arrangements had their attractions for honeymoon and other couples since there was plenty of room for two in the sunken bath, and Otani knew that most of the more expensive inns and hotels in hot-spring resorts offered them.

Earlier, while having his own bath, the rich red colour of the Arima water had been to Otani no more than a passing curiosity: in his time he had in various parts of Japan immersed himself from the neck down in green, sulphurous

17

yellow and murkily grey waters reputed to cure anything from cancer to piles or a sore throat. Now, however, the effect was gruesome in the extreme, because the bath was not only full, but occupied; by a man who was very obviously dead.

Chapter III

"It's a foreigner," Kimura said unnecessarily. Although the skin colour was not much swarthier than Otani's own, the features of the dead man's face were certainly not Japanese. Otani turned to the woman whom he now knew to be if not the proprietress at least the manageress of the hotel, since she had made a graciously ceremonious circuit of the Peony Room during their meal, speaking briefly to each guest. "There is no need at present to disturb any of the other police officers here tonight. Most are on the point of leaving anyway, and those who are staying should be treated like all your other guests. Please tell any of your staff who know anything about this to keep it to themselves. We'll come down to the lobby to talk to you again later." As he spoke Otani knew that such discretion was most unlikely to be achieved, but it was worth a try.

White-faced, the woman nodded and went away as Otani turned to Kimura and Migishima, suddenly incongruous in their yukatas. "You'd both better go and get dressed before

19

we do anything else," he suggested.

Kimura looked down at himself in some surprise. "Yes, I suppose we should," he agreed. "Back in five minutes." He was almost as good as his word, but even so, by the time he and Migishima returned, Otani and Noguchi between them had checked the bedroom and bathroom fairly thoroughly, and Otani was thoughtfully studying an Alien Registration Card.

"Hossein Fuhaido," he said carefully, reading the Japanese phonetic version of the man's name. "From the United Arab Emirates." Otani had heard of the country but had only the vaguest of ideas where it was. He handed the little green folder to Kimura, who looked at it himself. The late Hossein Fuhaid was, it seemed, 43 years old, a businessman, and lived in central Kobe.

"Wrists slashed," Otani went on. "No sign of a knife or razor, but it may be in the water. No suicide note, either." He rubbed his chin thoughtfully. "All right. We'll go down to the lobby, alert the duty officer at the Arima police station, organise an ambulance and have a preliminary word with the manageress or whoever she is. Migishima, get hold of a clean empty bottle and take a sample of the bath-water before it's drained away, would you?" Migishima paled a little but nodded manfully and disappeared as Otani raised his voice a little and turned to the open door of the bathroom. "Ninja! Do you mind hanging on here till we can get everything sorted out?" A muffled growl from within indicated assent and Otani and Kimura went out of the room, Kimura closing the door behind them.

Patrons of inns and hotels in Japanese hot-spring resorts are rarely night-owls, and the lobby was deserted apart from an elderly couple in their yukatas peering glumly at a modest display of souvenir trinkets in glass cases near a sales counter heaped with ready-wrapped boxes of cakes and other inexpensive presents for people to take home for friends and relatives. The counter was shrouded, and the lighting at the back of the lobby already dimmed for the night. It seemed that Otani's paradoxical instructions had been carried out, and that the considerable number of police officers under his command who had been boisterously in evidence a short time previously had either departed for home or gone to bed.

He nodded approvingly at the manageress as she emerged from behind the reception desk and bustled over to him and Kimura, no longer looking quite so shocked, but still flustered and wide-eyed. There were few types of experience which had not come her way during the course of her career in "the water business" as Japanese call every aspect of the entertainment and innkeeping trade, but the discovery of a body while the commander of a prefectural police force was actually on the premises was more than she was accustomed to cope with. She began to babble extravagant apologies, but Otani cut her off firmly and soon established that there was a service entrance to the hotel at the rear of the building. Then he went with her into her tiny office behind the reception area, leaving Kimura to arrange for an ambulance to be sent and to instruct the despatcher to persuade the crew to manage without the screaming of sirens as they approached the hotel.

It was obvious that outsiders were not expected to enter the office, which contained a small desk cluttered with folders and heaps of invoices, a chair, and not much else. Unperturbed, Otani sat on a sturdy cardboard carton in the corner containing half a dozen 1.8 litre bottles of his favourite "Gekkeikan" brand sake and waved the woman to the chair. "Officers from Arima police station will be taking full statements from you and other people here tomorrow," he said. "For the moment, just tell me what you know about the foreigner in that room upstairs. When did he check in?"

The manageress gulped audibly. "Well, you see, we offer a special—"

"When did he check in?"

"He arrived at about eleven-fifteen this morning, I believe."

Otani raised an eyebrow: guests are never expected to turn up at Japanese-style inns or hotels before late afternoon.

21

"This *morning*?"

The woman was clearly embarrassed. "Yes. I was just going to explain. We offer a lunchtime tariff between eleven in the morning and two in the afternoon for people visiting Arima for the day. They can take a bath and have a meal here at special cheap rates. Several other hotels here have very similar arrangements," she added defensively.

"I see. Usually couples, I presume. And you're not required to register them if they don't stay overnight, of course." Otani was not in the least shocked, but was somewhat surprised that a good-class and ostensibly respectable place should go in for such fringe activities as letting rooms by the hour during the day, however much economic sense it made. The woman said nothing: her heightened colour was itself eloquent. "So this man arrived with a companion?" There was a pause before Otani went on, his voice perceptibly harder. "Come, now. He must have done, or you wouldn't have put him in a room with its own bath."

"I wasn't on duty at the time," she said. "But yes. The day receptionist told me when I took over from her while she went to lunch that a foreign man and a woman were in Room 324."

As Otani shifted his position on the carton of sake there was a tap at the door, which was opened to reveal Kimura peering enquiringly round it. "Everything under control, Inspector?"

"Yes, sir."

"Good. I'll join you in the lobby in a moment." Otani stood up and gently massaged his backside as he looked down at the manageress. "I have things to do now. We shall also have a lot more questions to ask you. Do you live on the premises here?"

"Yes."

"Good. Please keep yourself available for the next hour or so. Just one more thing at this stage. Why was the room still occupied this evening if it had been booked only for a couple of hours at lunchtime?"

The woman still looked everywhere except directly at

Otani, but seemed to have recovered some of her former composure. Noticing this, he reflected that she was probably thinking with part of her mind that the death of a foreigner would almost certainly take priority, so far as the police were concerned, over any curiosity on their part about her bookkeeping arrangements, and that there would be plenty of time to tidy them up before they invited the tax authorities to look into them – if they ever got round to it.

"The guest rang down to reception towards two o'clock to say that he would like to keep the room for the rest of the day and evening. The receptionist checked with me and I talked to him myself. He spoke good Japanese but I was rather – well, he was a foreigner and everything and I wasn't sure about . . . anyway, he came down to the lobby and offered to pay cash for the full overnight rate in advance and we aren't very busy at present, so. . . "

"I see. But you still didn't ask him to register."

The manageress looked self-righteous: definitely a handsome, well-preserved woman, Otani thought. "He didn't *say* they wanted the room overnight."

"Never mind that for now. That was the first time you saw him yourself?"

"Yes."

"What about the woman? Did you see her?"

"No. He explained that they would be going out for a while later, but I took a couple of hours off duty because we had a busy evening ahead of us and they must have left during that time. I saw them come back, though – between four and four-thirty, I suppose it must have been. I happened to be behind the reception desk again. He picked up his key while the lady went into the ladies' room at the back of the lobby. I hardly saw her, really. The lift is very near the toilets and I didn't notice her go up."

Otani opened the door to go out, but hesitated before doing so. "She was Japanese, I presume?" The man whose corpse he had seen in the bath was not young. He was resident in Japan, and, as a businessman, probably well-to-do. He could most likely afford the services of a Japanese call-girl: might even belong to one of the new-style "love banks" which empanelled enthusiastic amateurs from the ranks of students, "office ladies" and young housewives with time on their hands and fixed them up with sugar daddies for a percentage of the hefty monthly fee such men stumped up with every evidence of enthusiasm.

"Oh, yes. I'd certainly have noticed if she'd been a foreigner."

Otani rubbed his eyes. What little effect the sake had had on him had already worn off, but he was more than ready for bed. "How did he seem when he came to reception to pay? Did you form any impression that he might be in an unusual state of mind?"

She shrugged. "It's hard to tell with foreigners. He seemed – oh, a bit embarrassed perhaps, but under the circumstances. . ."

"And when he came back later to pick up his key? Any difference?"

"Well, no. He didn't say a word. I recognised him, of course, so he didn't even have to mention the room number."

Otani stood there motionless and silent, maintaining the tension until the woman at last looked him in the eye. "And where is this woman now?" he enquired quietly then.

"I don't know," she replied. "Nobody saw her leave."

Chapter IV

"Brainy lad, young Hara," rumbled Inspector Ninja Noguchi as they awaited the arrival of the new head of the Criminal Investigation Section. Otani nodded his agreement, but nevertheless found himself rather wishing that they could do without him. He looked with affection from Noguchi to Kimura, the two colleagues on whom he really depended for support and advice.

It was a beautifully warm afternoon, and Otani had only just closed the windows of his big, shabby office in order to cut out some of the noise of the Kobe traffic. For the visit to Arima the previous day Noguchi had worn his only complete suit, plus the gaudy diamond-patterned cardigan he favoured during the chillier months of the year, but was now wearing his stained, frayed and once cream-coloured linen jacket over a shirt buttoned to the neck but without a tie, and his customary baggy trousers.

Kimura's clothes were in just as great a contrast to Otani's own tidy but nondescript dark "salaryman" suit, but in a quite

25

different way from Noguchi's. His sartorial tribute to the spring sunshine was a new casual jacket in soft wool of the palest grey-blue over a silk shirt and tie, and Italian trousers which he had been adjusting with minute care at the knee, revealing in the process a partially see-through grey silk sock with a crimson stripe up the side. Otani would have been astounded and horrified had he known that the whole carefully chosen ensemble had cost the best part of a month's salary: but then Kimura was a bachelor with nobody to spend his money on except himself and his women friends. Moreover, his well-to-do retired diplomat father was rumoured to subsidise him generously from the family coffers.

"Yes. Hara has obviously been putting in a certain amount of effort since he joined us," Kimura conceded graciously. "Let's hope it turns out to be constructive. He's late," he added, drawing back the cuff of his shirt and glancing at his watch. Otani noticed at once that it was yet another new one, but of a conventional, even old-fashioned design, quite unlike the latest examples of electronic gadgetry with numerous controls which normally took his fancy.

"New watch, Kimura-kun?" he enquired casually. Kimura beamed.

"The very latest thing, Chief. It's a modern replica of a watch marketed in the thirties. The gimmick is that there aren't any batteries to be replaced every year or so. You simply have to wind it up every night." Otani was nodding solemnly when there was a firm double knock on the door. "*Ohaeri nasai!*" Otani looked towards it as he responded, but noticed out of the corner of his eye that Kimura was winding his new watch surreptitiously and with some evidence of embarrassment.

"Sit down, Inspector. Thank you for joining us. Help yourself to some tea." Otani indicated the tray on the table with a wave of his hand, and watched as Hara poured himself a cup of green tea from the old tin kettle. The fourth easy chair round the low coffee table was rarely occupied, and the room suddenly struck Otani as being overcrowded. Kimura had drawn back a little into his own customary territory, and only Noguchi seemed to be not only completely at ease but even to be regarding Hara with a kind of fatherly indulgence.

"You've been with us now for, what is it, just over a month, Inspector. I expect you know that in addition to our regular formal staff meetings involving all heads of sections I confer frequently with Inspectors Noguchi and Kimura. Mr Kimura was acting commander during a period I was away in England a year or so ago. I'm sorry to have dragged you all here on a Saturday afternoon, but I think we ought to talk about two new cases which present puzzling features – three if one includes the alleged rape at the Kobe Women's Junior College – "

"Which happens to adjoin the premises of the mosque just off Tor Road, Commander. The Islamic thread running through these incidents does indeed leap to one's notice."

"I haven't quite finished what I was going to say, Inspector." Otani's voice was quiet and friendly, but firm, and Kimura shot a satisfied look at Noguchi, who had however closed his eyes as he usually did during conferences.

"The Moslem community in Kobe is not very large, and has over the years been peaceable and unobtrusive. Yet suddenly within a matter of days one of its members has been killed in a hit-and-run road accident, another is alleged to have raped a nineteen-year old student, and a third has been found dead at the Grand View Hotel in Arima in circumstances which suggest suicide but which have yet to be clarified."

"The hit-and-run has to have been a contract," Noguchi said, opening his eyes briefly. Ninja Noguchi knew more about the seedy underbelly of Kobe society than all the rest of them put together, since his constituency of small-time crooks, hoodlums and drug-pushers took in particularly the waterfront area and the cheap bars which were not too particular to welcome deckhands from freighters who represented every human colour and creed, including Islam. His involvement in the investigation was essential.

So was Kimura's. In spite of his nonchalant approach to his

27

duties he was a man with flair, and above all a man who understood much more clearly than the great majority of Japanese what made foreigners tick. Otani himself found Kimura's taste for their society incomprehensible, but was grateful for it because of the insights it seemed to provide into the ways of the considerable expatriate minority living in his jurisdiction.

It remained to be seen whether Hara would have more to contribute than his predecessor, the unlamented Sakamoto, whose idea of investigating a crime was to round up everyone in sight and interrogate them until somebody or other confessed out of sheer boredom. At least, this was how Kimura had once described Sakamoto's methods to Otani, who recalled his words now as he sat and stared at the gloomy oil painting on the wall and waited for one of his lieutenants to say something else.

It seemed that his quiet rebuke had silenced Hara for the time being, because it was Kimura who spoke next. His manner when he did so was thoughtful, almost academic. "The real problem is that all these Moslems hate each other. I always think there's nothing like religion for bringing out the worst in people. Christians are pretty notorious, but I really think Moslems are worse. Look at Lebanon."

Otani interrupted. "I think you've got that wrong, Kimura. It was the Israelis, surely, who . . . they aren't Moslems, are they?"

He wasn't absolutely sure, and was relieved when Kimura waved a hand airily. "No, no, of course not, they're Jews. But you get my point."

"What point? You're talking rubbish." This time it was Noguchi who rumbled an objection, seemingly to his own surprise, since he opened his eyes wide, looked round and then closed them again, reverting to his usual massive immobility.

Kimura now adopted an air of ostentatious patience, like a schoolmaster faced with a particularly dense collection of pupils. "What I am trying to get across to you is that Islam has in recent years become a very militant religion. Moslems belong to all sorts of different countries, and most of them are at daggers drawn with each other. What's more, every group claims to be more Islamic than the next lot. So forget about Lebanon for a minute. We've had the Iranians at war with the Iraqis, Sadat of Egypt assassinated, that fellow Gaddafi in Libya – "

"So what?" This time Noguchi's eyes remained closed, but one large hand moved up and rasped over the stubble of his battered face. "Let's hear what Hara has to say." Kimura relapsed into an offended silence as Hara stirred in his seat. Otani waited with some interest for his contribution, having not really grasped what Kimura had been driving at either.

Otani read the Mainichi newspaper every day, finding the Asahi rather too highbrow for him, and even occasionally discussed the international scene with Hanae, but on the whole found quite enough to think about in reflecting on Hyogo prefecture and its problems. He had a soft spot for Britain now that he and Hanae had been there to visit their daughter, her businessman husband and their small son who was the Otanis' only grandchild and the apple of their eye, but the rest of the world bored him. Certainly Otani could not pretend to more than the vaguest notion of the nature of the disagreeable events he gathered took place on a regular basis in the Middle East.

Replacing the glasses he had been polishing, and blinking and twitching as he did so, Hara nevertheless spoke in measured, considered tones. "I believe the Inspector is right in putting forward the hypothesis that the Kobe Mosque may usefully be considered as a microcosm or perhaps analogue of the Islamic world. Theoretically it is open to all Moslems, no matter whether they are Shia or Sunni; or indeed adhere to other, smaller sects. For your added information, sir, I should explain that Moslems of any nationality may attend the weekly prayer meeting, provided only of course that they are male. No woman may enter the central part of a mosque."

"Exactly what I was saying," Kimura pointed out in a

29

wounded way.

Otani perked up. "Is that so? I read a *misteri* novel once where this woman dressed herself up as a man to get at her victim. It wasn't a mosque though, it was one of those clubs in London where they don't let women in. I wonder if perhaps some Moslem woman might have killed that fellow at Arima and made it look like suicide . . . she could have made herself up to look Japanese. You can get these wigs in department stores . . ."

They all waited as Otani's brief flight of fancy fizzled out. "We can't rule it out, Chief," Kimura said kindly. "I think what we seem to be agreed on at the outset, though, is that there must be quite a bit of tension among the various factions the members of the mosque community belong to. Some of it arising from religious differences, some because of their various nationalities."

"I don't see what you mean by religious differences if they're all Moslems."

"Hara just explained, didn't he?" It was unheard of for Noguchi to take an interest in so recondite a subject. Moreover, although his age and the intimacy of their association licensed him to be blunt with Otani, his remark came perilously close to the permitted limit, and Otani looked at him sharply as Kimura went on with careful patience.

"It's like Buddhism really. You know, there's Tendai, and Zen, and, er – "

"Shingon, and Jodo Shin, and Nichiren – " Kimura did not look grateful for Hara's helpful additions to the litany of the names of sects. Otani cut in. "Yes, yes, but nobody gets excited about the differences. Most of us haven't got the slightest idea what they are. Except Nichiren, I suppose."

"Ah, there you are. We all know that Nichiren people are rather fanatical and intolerant. Well, there are Moslems like that. That old man Khomeini in Iran, for one." Kimura sat back in some exhaustion after his sustained effort to outdo the learned Hara.

"All right. I take your point." Otani reached forward, poured himself another cup of tepid tea and drank it down, grimacing at its bitterness. He was getting tired of religion, and Noguchi seemed to have gone quite decisively to sleep following his unexpected intervention. "The Islamic community in Kobe amount to a mixed bag, and the two men might have had a variety of enemies among them."

Noguchi was not asleep. He shifted perhaps an inch in his chair, with an effect as of a violent convulsion. "Suppose the Arima guy just did himself in? That's what it looks like. Why make it complicated?"

Otani decided to assert his authority as chairman. "That's a key question, Ninja. Still no suicide note, and no idea who the woman was who went to the hotel with him. Just one of those knives in the water with the snap-off angled blades you can buy in any hardware shop. There must be millions of them in tool-boxes and kitchen drawers up and down the country. Oh, yes, there are a lot of enquiries to be made about that fellow's background, and the other one's too. The one killed in the street. All the same, I thought it might be worth while to run them in parallel, just to see whether the two men had anything in common apart from their religion, and if so, what. Maybe you'd better start a joint file and see if any coincidences crop up."

Kimura was offended. "I've already done it," he protested. "I've prepared a summary." He picked up a plain folder he had placed on the brown linoleum beside his chair and took out some photocopied sheets, passing one each to Otani and Noguchi and then with some reluctance handing one to Hara, who blinked with redoubled fury as he scrutinised it.

The information was neatly set out in tabular form, with the many foreign words written in Roman script accompanied by transliterations into Japanese phonetic characters. The information was in three columns, thus:

31

NAME	Ahmed el Abdalla	Hossein Al Fuhaid
NATIONALITY	Sudanese	UAE
AGE	34	43
PROFESSION	Lecturer in Agricultural Engineering, University of Khartoum	Shipping agent
STATUS IN JAPAN	Visiting Research Fellow Kobe University	Residence permit for business purposes
MARITAL STATUS	Married (wife + two children in Sudan)	Divorced

Otani sucked his teeth thoughtfully as he studied the sheet, but Noguchi was more immediate in his reaction. "Took you long enough to put this together," he grumbled.

Kimura sniffed haughtily in his direction. "Oh, really, Ninja. Do be reasonable. I've had quite a busy morning, I assure you. This is just the bare bones for ease of reference."

"Go ahead, we're listening," Otani said quietly, and Kimura produced more sheets from his folder: notes to which he referred from time to time.

"Abdalla arrived in Japan only very recently, financed by a grant from the Japanese government payable through the Japan Society for the Promotion of Science. Fuhaid, on the other hand, had been here for nearly three years, working with a small shipping company involved with trade from Japan to the Gulf ports. It's a Japanese company but they successfully argued to the Ministry of Justice that they needed an Arabic speaker to handle correspondence in that language, so he got a residence visa and work permit without too much trouble. So. Two men with totally different professional backgrounds and different nationalities."

He shuffled through his notes. "If Fuhaid had been another Sudanese or even an Egyptian, there might have been some political link."

As Kimura briefly hesitated, Hara piped up again. "Very true, sir. The Sudanese Republic is in effect the only other

32

Islamic country in the Middle East which remains on reasonable terms with Egypt since they established diplomatic relations with the Israelis, and for your added information – "

Otani cut him off impatiently. "We've been through all that before. Do get on, Kimura."

"Sorry, Chief. Well, as you see, Fuhaid was divorced. Abdalla had a wife and children back home. We don't yet know if Fuhaid made a regular practice of visiting the mosque or whether he'd ever met Abdalla. The big day of the week for Moslems is Friday, and if our friend preferred to spend it having fun and games with a girlfriend it suggests to me that he wasn't a very pious soul."

"That's one of the oddest things about it," Otani cut in. "I should have thought that a man in a suicidal frame of mind is hardly likely to start the day in the way that this fellow seems to have done."

Kimura nodded in agreement. "Right. Very peculiar. All the same, I'm disinclined to think the two incidents are connected, and I certainly can't see any possible link with the rape affair."

"Inspector Hara. Your people are looking into that. Any progress? Do you agree with Inspector Kimura?"

"I called on the Imam – that is to say priest or spiritual director of the mosque yesterday following the death of Dr el Abdalla, sir. The appointment had in fact been made previously, since I had intended to ask him in confidence whether he might have any idea which if any of the members of his congregation might be able to assist our enquiries into the alleged rape."

Kimura bristled, largely for form's sake, since he had learned of the fact from Migishima the previous evening at Arima. "Indeed? I thought it was understood that contact with foreigners is the responsibility of my section," he snapped.

Otani wheeled round in his chair and glared at him, then at Hara and Noguchi in turn. "Understand this, gentlemen. I will tolerate no childish squabbling over spheres of interest.

This headquarters is very far from being overstaffed, and there is plenty for all of you to do without getting under each other's feet. When we are working together on an investigation like this, however, I expect *friendly cooperation* among you. A little good-natured chaffing is one thing, but . . ." He simmered down and resumed his usual quiet style. "I apologise for raising my voice. What did this Imam have to say, Hara?"

Hara's ungainly body was contorted in embarrassment. "Sir. He's a scholarly old gentleman who speaks excellent Japanese. We had a fascinating conversation about the theological implications of his presiding over such a variegated congregation. He was of course greatly distressed by the death a short time previously in such circumstances of Dr el Abdalla . . ."

Mesmerised by Hara's flickering eyelids, Otani took off his own glasses and rubbed his eyes. He had been finding it more difficult to cope with fine print lately and thought he might have to go along to the optical department store for a free test and a new lens prescription which they would make up for him there and then. "He'd met Abdalla, then?"

"Yes, sir. The man appears even in such a short time to have made his presence felt at the mosque. I inferred from what the Imam said that Abdalla was an officious sort of man, eager to serve on committees, be given some kind of petty authority. In short, over-anxious to be helpful."

"The Imam didn't take to him." That much Otani had grasped.

"It would appear not, sir. Needless to say, though, he had not actually witnessed the incident and was clearly not suspicious about the circumstances or the possibility of deliberate homicide. Nor, for your added information, could he help in the matter of the rape."

Kimura joined in cautiously, chastened by Otani's tongue-lashing which he knew quite well had been intended for him. "I'd like to suggest that Hara's people should begin by questioning Fuhaid's Japanese business colleagues on

Monday, sir. See if they might be able to throw any light on his state of mind. If it's agreeable I'd like to talk to people at the University who knew Abdalla – and the man who identified him at the scene yesterday. He's obviously a regular member of the mosque congregation. A Pakistani, it seems."

"That seems reasonable." Otani looked at Noguchi. "Not a lot for you at the moment, Ninja, I'm afraid. Except that you're pretty sure the hit-and-run was a contract job?"

Noguchi took in a vast quantity of air. "That's what I said. Had a look at the photos. Interesting skid-marks. Traffic people agree."

"I presume you've put the word out to some of your contacts?" Noguchi nodded with his habitual economy of movement, and Otani rose to his feet, the others following suit.

"Good. We'll meet again on Monday or Tuesday." He moved towards the door with his colleagues, and put a hand on Kimura's arm to hold him back after the other two went out. "By the way, how did you find out all that political stuff about the Middle East? I didn't know you took any interest in that kind of thing." From Kimura's guilty but defiant look as he reacted to the question Otani guessed at once that there was a woman in it somewhere. He was right.

"Well, actually, I've become acquainted with a rather interesting Jewish girl recently," Kimura confessed. "She's extremely knowledgeable about all sorts of things. . ."

Chapter V

Shulamit Steiner was not only knowledgeable about the politics of the Islamic world and of the Middle East in particular: she was also a striking-looking woman, and Kimura gazed at her fondly as they sat in the American-style saloon called The Attic at the top of a restored building dating from the nineteenth century. Faced with wood and embellished with wrought-iron railings, it is known as the Ijinkan or Foreigners' Hall, and sits at the heart of the oldest residential quarter, nowadays promoted by the Kobe city fathers as a tourist attraction.

Kimura liked The Attic with its irregularly angled ceiling and haphazard collection of ephemera from the America of the fifties and sixties, the functioning juke-box, the car licence plates from Nevada and Wyoming, the tattered posters advertising James Dean and Marlon Brando movies, and the dusty panties, bras and collegiate pennants with which the walls were festooned. He had discovered the place long before, and much admired its American owner's easy, friendly manner, youthful good looks and casually stylish dress, not to mention the relaxed and natural way in which he spoke Japanese. Kimura preferred to practise his English with him, though, and had chatted to him on a number of occasions, often about baseball, learning a number of pleasing up-to-date colloquialisms which he rehearsed in private and reproduced on subsequent occasions.

It was warm in there and Shulamit shrugged off her jacket, under which she was wearing a plain T-shirt. She had a lean, wiry body: almost painfully thin, but her face was vibrant with life, her features exotically attractive to Kimura. For Shulamit was a quarter Japanese and had inherited from her grandfather an oriental delicacy of bone structure and a wondrous complexion. Yet there was nothing Japanese about her eyes, which were big, greenish-grey and lustrous, nor about the silky, flaming red hair which was that evening piled up loosely on her head. "It's set for Saturday," she said in reply to a question he had put to her earlier. "Frankly, they bore the pants off me, but I have to go."

"I met you at one of them in the first place," Kimura pointed out, slightly offended. "Personally, I'm quite grateful to the Kinki International Students' Society."

Shulamit twisted her lips in an appealing grin. "I just love that wild name, don't you? My folks thought I was kidding when I mentioned it once in a letter." Then she reached out across the dark wooden surface of the table and patted his hand. "Don't get me wrong, Jiro. You're the greatest pick-up I've made since I hit town last fall."

Shulamit had seemed moody and out of sorts when she arrived twenty minutes late at The Attic where Kimura had been waiting for her, but food and drink seemed to have cheered her up, and now her smile was warm and encouraging. Kimura squeezed the hand which was still in his, at the same time nudging her leg with his own under the table. "Pick-up hell," he protested in a good-humoured way. "I'm not in the habit of getting picked up. I picked *you* up. Offered you my own helping of smoked salmon, if I remember rightly.

Also, I'm not too sure about the way you put that. 'The greatest pick-up'? One of a number, am I?"

Shulamit smiled again, stuck the tip of her tongue out at him lasciviously, then pursed her lips into a kiss which she actually leaned across and delivered to Kimura. The patrons of The Attic are mostly young and the atmosphere is free and easy, but this was still Japan, and Kimura glanced round in some confusion before looking again at Shulamit who was grinning at him broadly. "Hey, what happened to my laid-back Jiro? Relax, honey. You're among friends." Kimura smiled sheepishly as the American girl seized his hand again.

"Let's just say that this particular graduate student of sociology decided you were the best prospect she'd seen to date on or off campus, shall we?" Although Kimura had known for two or three years of the existence of KISS, as the Kinki International Students' Society was invariably called by its members, he had never attended any of its functions. Then his attention had been caught by an announcement in the English-language *Mainichi Daily News* that an "International Goodwill Party" would be held to mark the New Year at the newspaper's headquarters building in downtown Osaka, a mere half-hour away on the interurban train and constituting with Kobe and Kyoto and their environs the so-called Kinki area, the densely populated focus of the larger Kansai region of western Japan. KISS members were to be the guests, and internationally minded but non-student Japanese were invited to participate at a charge per person of three thousand yen, a tidy sum but no more than the cost of a Western-style dinner in a hotel restaurant.

Quite apart from being ever mindful of his official duty to keep an unobtrusive eye on them, Kimura liked to be in the swim where foreigners were concerned. He sometimes felt he knew too little about the motley collection of overseas students in the numerous national, prefectural, municipal and private universities in the area, who in any case seldom stayed for more than a year or so. He had therefore gone along to the International Goodwill Party looking forward to

38

airing his excellent English and to taking the pulse of the younger element in the foreign community.

Kimura had from time to time in the course of his strenuous amorous career made passes at attractive foreign girl students who crossed his path, but on the whole he was rather chary of women with intellectual interests. For the most part he preferred to pursue those who turned up in Kobe at fairly frequent intervals as members of the consular corps or secretaries working for foreign companies. Furthermore, he was usually attracted to foreign women with generous physical endowments: in his experience Japanese women were usually generously cooperative and often quite inventive in bed, but rarely looked beautiful in the nude.

For all her scrawny body, though, Shulamit Steiner was something special. She had stood out like a beacon against the background of her fellow foreigners at the New Year party, and not only because of her extraordinary hair. There was an assurance and a vitality emanating from her which had attracted Kimura very strongly, and he had been even more impressed when he drifted over to her vicinity and heard her speaking in heavily accented but good Japanese to an elderly professor who was looking distinctly overwhelmed, and who made off with every appearance of relief when Kimura caught her eye and butted in to introduce himself.

The smoked salmon episode proved to be the beginning of a relationship which developed rapidly. Kimura had been carrying a plateful with the intention of eating it himself, but Shulamit pounced on it with glee. "Terrific! How did you guess? Genuine kosher food at last! Hey, you're not Jewish, are you?"

"You didn't seriously think I might be Jewish, did you?" Kimura now asked.

"Grow up, Jiro, of course not. Mind you, I've met some Japanese Jews. Women who converted when they married foreign men. With my background, that doesn't seem so wild to me as it probably does to you. Did you know there've been Chinese Jews since the sixteenth century?"

Although Kimura had in the three months or so of their acquaintance listened more or less attentively to Shulamit's frequent homilies about Judaism he felt that on the whole he could manage without an explanation of the Chinese connection. He was hoping to persuade her to accompany him back to his flat later and had every intention of steering the conversation into more romantic channels before long, but wanted to clear up the matter of the next regular get-together of KISS members first. "Really? I'll be darned," he said perfunctorily. "That's really fascinating. Next Saturday, you say? Where's it going to be? Will you be going?"

Shulamit looked at him through half-closed eyes. "Next Saturday. Five p.m., would you believe it? A hell of a time to have a party. Back in Chicago I'm just about getting out of *bed* at five in the afternoon, for God's sake." Kimura was much affected by the lingering stress Shulamit placed on the word "bed" and took a particularly deep breath. "They've fixed it up at Doshisha Women's College in Kyoto this time. These private colleges have pretty good facilities: better than the national universities. And more money to spend. I doubt there'll be smoked salmon, though. It's just as well I have permission to eat non-kosher food while I'm in Japan."

"You're going, then? All the way to Kyoto?"

Shulamit's grey-green eyes flashed. "Going? You bet I'm going, buster. Do you know the Islamic group tried to get all Jewish members of KISS thrown out not too long ago? When they didn't get their way they threatened to boycott meetings. That didn't work either, so now they're trying to squeeze us out any way they can. There are only six of us around at the moment, but I'm telling you there'll be six of us there in Kyoto on Saturday."

Kimura had long since finished his beer and watched while Shulamit drained the last of hers. "Why are you so interested anyway? Want me to take you along as a guest?"

Kimura had not mentioned at their first meeting that he was a police officer. Their conversation had centred first on pleased surprise at discovering that they had both been born

40

in Chicago, where Kimura's father had served as a vice-consul until the attack on Pearl Harbor and to which he had returned with his wife and son for several years as Japanese Consul-General when diplomatic relations were restored. Then they had moved on to Shulamit's research, towards a Ph.D. thesis to be entitled *Gender Identification and Sex Role Reversal among Japanese Women*. The word "sex" always made Kimura perk up, and he had been intrigued to learn that Shulamit was engaged on a study of the attitudes of members of the renowned Takarazuka All-Girl Revue company whose base is not far from Kobe.

It was not until their first evening out together, at the Duke of Wellington English-style pub-restaurant in Tor Road that Kimura casually announced that he was in fact an inspector on the staff of Hyogo Prefectural Police Headquarters, and felt more than a little disappointed by Shulamit's matter-of-fact response. She had seemed curiously unimpressed and neither surprised nor intrigued as other foreign women tended to be on discovering his profession.

"I might go with you," he now said nonchalantly. "If I have the time. You think the Arab and other Moslem students will be there, then? The boycott idea is off?"

"You seem very interested all of a sudden, Jiro. Why the big concern with Moslems? Isn't a nice Jewish girl good enough for you?"

Kimura hesitated a moment, and then treated Shulamit to one of his most winsome smiles. "I can't fool you, can I? I *am* interested, yes. A Sudanese researcher was killed in a traffic accident yesterday afternoon, and in the evening another Arab died in a hotel at Arima Onsen. Two dead Moslems in our jurisdiction in one day. It's just a funny coincidence, of course, but it's intriguing all the same."

Shulamit bent down and picked up her handbag, rummaged in it and found a small make-up mirror into which she peered and pulled a face. "That so? I hadn't heard. How did the second guy die?" she said then, putting the mirror back and snapping the bag shut decisively.

"We're not sure yet. Might have been suicide. It will have been on Kansai TV news this evening, and there'll be something in the local paper tomorrow, I expect."

"Well, you're welcome to come with me next week if you want to sniff around the survivors, but don't expect me to introduce you. Come on, let's go." She went ahead out of the door while Kimura paid the bill for their barbecued chicken and beer. Shulamit seemed to have adequate funds: enough to enable her to rent a one-room apartment within easy commuting distance of Kobe University rather than live in a overseas students' dormitory, anyway. All the same, she always let Kimura pay when they went out to eat together.

Once outside the Ijinkan and in the street Shulamit tucked her arm firmly under Kimura's and he was pleasantly conscious of the warmth of her body against him, but it was not until they were rounding the corner near the Kobe Club that either of them spoke again. "I guess they'll show up on Saturday OK," Shulamit then said abruptly, stopping short so that Kimura almost lost his footing. "If you're involved in the paperwork over those two deaths maybe you *should* go to Kyoto with me at that. You might pick up some talk." In the artificial street lighting her eyes as she gazed into Kimura's looked black, and this all at once made her seem much more Japanese. "Why aren't you sure about the suicide?"

"I don't know really," Kimura admitted ruefully. "People planning to kill themselves often choose to go to hotels, but generally leave a note or something. He didn't. I'd like to find out if his acquaintances knew of anything that might have been bothering him badly enough. I imagine it won't take long for the news to spread around the Moslem community, though, from what you tell me about the various intrigues among them, some of them might have been pleased rather than sorry to hear that he's dead."

The deaths of Dr el Abdalla and Hossein Fuhaid seemed likely to arouse a flurry of media interest, both local and possibly national. The patrolman at the nearby police box had reported that Press and TV photographers had been seen outside the Kobe Mosque during the day, and Kimura was fairly confident that even though the rape allegation had not been publicised, lubricious attention would inevitably be drawn to the fact that the building was located next to the Kobe Women's Junior College dormitory, separated only by a parking lot at the rear of which was the single-storey Arabic Institute and language school attached to the mosque.

Kimura had insufficiently wound up his new wristwatch that afternoon in Otani's office, so he took out a recently acquired ball-point pen which featured a digital time-display at one end as well as playing a catchy tune at noon and "Auld Lang Syne", immensely popular in Japan, at midnight. It wasn't too easy to read the time in the street-lighting, but he decided that it must be eight thirty-four. "It's still early," he said. "Would you care to come back to my place for a drink?"

Shulamit was only an inch or so shorter than he was, and looked him in the eye in a very friendly way. "Gee, I thought you'd never ask," she said, with that touch of huskiness that Kimura always noticed in her voice when she was in the mood for sex. "Listen though, I have to be over at Takarazuka by nine in the morning to talk to somebody there. So just a quick screw, then I have to go get some sleep. Okay?" Not for the first time, Kimura was both stimulated and gratified by Shulamit's forthright refusal to beat about the bush. He thought he might invite himself along to Takarazuka with her. The next day was after all a Sunday, and there was no sense in working all weekend.

Chapter VI

"Part of the trouble," Otani said reflectively to Hanae, "is the way he looks. He wears those glasses with the round metal frames like the ones they used to issue during the war. And he's awkward and blinks all the time, and he never stops lecturing people." He carefully laid a wafer of processed seaweed on the flat oblong platter in front of him, placed a pungent leaf of the *shiso* plant on top of it, and then with his chopsticks selected a choice slice of bream which he put on the leaf. Adding a morsel of pink pickled ginger, he rolled his creation up into a neat cylinder and popped it into his mouth whole as Hanae watched indulgently.

"Glasses like that are quite fashionable again now," she pointed out. "John Lennon used to wear them." She smiled at the bafflement in her husband's face. "You remember. One of the *Biitoruzu*. The one who married Mr Ono's niece." Otani nodded. He did remember, especially the lurid accounts in the Japanese press of the fuss the wealthy and well-connected Ono family made at the time.

The Otanis usually ordered ready-made sushi from a shop not far from where they lived in suburban Rokko and had it delivered by the assistant on his motor scooter, but that April evening they were enjoying instead a meal of sashimi, Hanae having brought the sliced raw fish home with her from a department store in Kobe. "It does sound as if Inspector Hara looks rather odd, though," Hanae agreed, adjusting the neckline of her yukata. They had both had their evening baths, and though the nights were still on the chilly side it was quite warm enough in the old wooden house nestling near the foothills of Mount Rokko for them to be able to sit comfortably in the downstairs room in their blue and white patterned kimono-style cotton wrappers.

Otani reached for the sake flask and refilled Hanae's tiny cup and his own much larger one. "He's an improvement on Sakamoto, needless to say, even if he does keep saying 'for your added information'," he conceded, and sipped the warm liquor as he mused briefly on the abrupt departure from the Hyogo force of Hara's predecessor and its extraordinary aftermath. Then he shook his head and rubbed his swarthy face as though brushing away a physical irritant.

"And strangely enough he seems to get along quite well with Ninja of all people." Inspector Hara was one of the new breed of fast-stream university graduate police officers, and Otani was indeed observing with curiosity and some amusement the emergence of an embryonic alliance between him and the scruffy, battered, streetwise Noguchi. "Perhaps it's because Ninja hardly ever talks and Hara never stops. All the same, Kimura doesn't seem to be able to hit it off with him, and there are silly squabbles beginning already about who does what. It's nice to have Japanese food again," he added carefully.

For the previous few weeks Hanae had been attending another series of classes in Western-style cookery at the Kobe YWCA and had not only been presenting her husband in the evenings with far more exotic sauces and potatoes in various guises than he really cared for, but had even on two occasions given him sandwiches with strangely compounded fillings to take to the office for his lunch in place of his usual lacquer lunch box full of cold cooked rice, pickles and assorted tit-bits of fish, chicken and vegetables.

Hanae took the hint, but said nothing. During their eventful visit to England, her husband had tucked into the most extraordinary mountains of alien food with a gusto which had astounded her, but on returning to Japan had at once reverted to his former preferences, even looking dubiously at the genuine English-style pork pie she had thought to please him by buying from the delicatessen in Kobe a few weeks after their return.

In any case, she was enjoying their supper that evening too, especially the taste of the bream; rather more than that of the deep red flesh of the tuna which made up the selection on the dish between them. With her chopsticks she took a piece for herself before her husband ate it all, dipping it delicately in her little dish of soy sauce. "What have you decided to do, then?" she asked when it had been disposed of.

Otani sighed unconvincingly. "Take charge of the cases myself, I'm afraid. It's the only way out."

Hanae wasted no words in commiserating with her husband over the latest addition to his burden of responsibility. They had been married for many years and she recognised very well the look she now saw in his eyes and the ill-concealed relish with which he seized on any and every chance to involve himself in operational work rather than sticking to his administrative and public-relations chores.

Otani maintained his expression of false gloom. "It will help to take my mind off this wretched development project, too." For years the Otanis had watched with regret the inexorable advance of the rash of speculative building spreading all over what had been the comparatively sparsely developed Rokko foothills, changing what Otani remembered from his boyhood as a village quite distinct from the city of Kobe into an increasingly crowded dormitory suburb. They had taken comfort from the steepness of the shaggy

46

folds of Mount Rokko which at once protected their old wooden house and seemed to scorn the ravages of the violators of the coastal plain; but times and techniques were changing. The municipal authorities had literally moved a mountain to build Port Island with its international conference centre, huge hotel, blocks of flats and impressive hospital, and were repeating the process to create Rokko Island in plain view from the fine room upstairs in which the Otanis slept and received formally their very occasional guests.

All that was bad enough, but even nearer to their house unmitigated disaster threatened. A developer with what Otani knew to be right-wing political and gangster connections had quite legally acquired a substantial tract of hitherto undeveloped hillside no more than a few hundred metres from their house. He now proposed to gouge great terraces out of it on which to build several blocks of "mansion" flats, most of which would overlook the Otanis and their few existing neighbours.

Hanae had become much more active in the neighbourhood association and had even gone so far as to establish contact with the fledgling environmental conservation movement in Kobe, whose young and enthusiastic members were to be seen every Sunday in the busiest shopping areas of the city drumming up signatures to a petition addressed to the Governor of Hyogo Prefecture and the Mayor of Kobe urging them to block the scheme. Otani, for his part, had buttonholed some of the more influential of his fellow members of the Kobe South Rotary Club. They both knew in their hearts that money talks in modern Japan, though, and had no real hope of success. It was Hanae's turn to sigh, but then she firmly redirected the conversation. "It was fortunate that the Migishimas happened to be passing by. You don't know for sure that the driver of the taxi *intended* to kill that poor man, though. And as for the suicide. . ."

Otani had been too tired on his return from Arima late on the previous Friday evening to tell Hanae about the discovery of Fuhaid's body, had spent much of Saturday at his office and been thoughtful and uncommunicative over the rest of the weekend. Now it was Monday, though, and earlier in the evening he had told Hanae about the deaths of the two Moslems while she was washing his back for him in their tiny bathroom; an indulgence to which he was treated much less often than he would have liked in recent years, but at any rate a lot more frequently than he was permitted to return the compliment by washing Hanae's. Since becoming a grandmother she had decided that it was really rather indecorous for the two of them to fool about together in the nude like a pair of honeymooners, however many compliments her husband paid her on her nowadays plumper but still firm and shapely body.

Otani shook his head briefly. "Well, it wasn't entirely a coincidence that they happened to be there. The story I heard from Kimura was that Junko-san – Migishima's wife – was rather put out by the fact that Hara had kept her on the fringes of the investigation of the rape at the Kobe Women's College dormitory, on the grounds that anything to do with Moslems is a job for men only. I think I mentioned that the girl claims that the man who attacked her looked like an Arab and made off into the grounds of the mosque. Anyway, last Friday both the Migishimas happened to be off duty, so she dragged her husband up there to look around a bit for herself. I suspect that she had taken the trouble to find out that their weekly prayer meeting starts at 12.30 on Fridays."

Hanae smiled. "That sounds like her." Hanae often savoured the recollection of her triumph on the Migishimas' wedding day, and made a point of enquiring about the wellbeing of the young couple from time to time.

"Well, she and Migishima both showed considerable presence of mind," Otani continued, constructing another seaweed and raw fish roll as he spoke, but this time before eating it dipping one end into his own dish of soy sauce, which was strongly seasoned with fierce green Japanese horseradish paste.

48

Hanae realised as she saw Otani's eyes glaze over that he had firmly concluded that the two deaths were linked and had drifted off into speculation about motive, method and opportunity. He was an avid reader of *misteri* novels, even though he sometimes flung down the one he was reading in scorn, exclaiming bitterly that it would be very nice indeed if things worked out so neatly in real life. Philosophically Hanae cleared away the supper dishes and left Otani to his reverie, but with a replenished flask of freshly warmed sake in front of him: she had never known him to become so absorbed that he forgot to refill his cup at regular intervals. There was little in the way of dish-washing to be done, and within ten minutes she had tidied the kitchen and was about to go back into the all-purpose downstairs living-room when all at once the door-bell rang.

This was a most unusual occurrence in the evening, and for a fraction of a second it was as though an icy finger clutched at Hanae's heart as she remembered the occasion during one of Otani's absences when she had been overpowered and abducted by an evening caller. Then she relaxed as she heard her husband's calm, reassuring voice. "Stay where you are, Ha-chan. I'll answer it." Then followed the sound of the old-fashioned screw-bolt and the rattle of the sliding door being opened, and, to Hanae's great surprise, the sound of Inspector Kimura's voice apologising effusively to Otani for disturbing him.

"Well, you've done it now, so you might as well come in and have a drink," Hanae heard her husband say in the good-humoured but ironical style he usually reserved for Kimura, and gazed at herself in dismay in the small mirror on the kitchen wall. Although she tut-tutted dutifully whenever Otani told her about Kimura's latest amorous escapade, Hanae had a very soft spot for him and had no intention of allowing him to see her without at least a trace of make-up, still less with nothing on under her yukata. As soon as she heard the two men go into the living-room, Hanae fled upstairs and made the necessary adjustments to her appearance as quickly as she could before descending again with great dignity, kneeling and bowing low in welcome to their guest. Kimura hastily scrambled to his knees and followed suit, and they exchanged courtesies as Otani looked on with a hint of impatience.

"I've offered Kimura-san some sake, but I think he'd probably prefer some of that Scotch whisky. There's some left, isn't there? You'd like a whisky, Kimura-kun?" After a great show of reluctance Kimura finally admitted that he would, and Hanae brought the half-full bottle of Old Parr, a glass, some water and ice, subjecting Jiro Kimura to a thorough scrutiny as she set the tray down on the tatami matting and took her time over transferring its contents to the low table at which he was now sitting. He smiled his thanks at her as he spoke, and Hanae once again thought she could understand the reactions of the women, both Japanese and foreign, who fell for him with such monotonous regularity.

"I was just explaining to the Superintendent that I ought of course to have telephoned, but I was up at the University just ten minutes walk away from here and thought you might forgive me if I were to look in." As she was hastening to assure him of their pleasure in his unexpected visit, Hanae was relieved to see that the twinkle was as noticeable as ever in his bright black eyes and that Kimura looked fit and lively, notwithstanding his demarcation dispute with the erudite Inspector Hara.

"You make me feel guilty. Sitting here relaxing while you've been working. Go on, put a bit more whisky in your glass. That's much too weak," Otani insisted. Although her husband had in recent years taken to discussing police matters with her more and more, Hanae knew that it would never do to make the fact obvious to Kimura. She therefore slipped unobtrusively out of the room and ensconced herself in the kitchen where she took down and opened a newly acquired, profusely illustrated book on Western-style cookery: in spite of her husband's unsubtle remark she was minded to have a go at duck with orange sauce some time in the near future.

The fact that the men's voices were clearly audible in the kitchen did not, she thought defiantly, make her an eavesdropper.

"What took you to the University?"

"I dropped in at the administration office to ask about Abdalla and go through their list of overseas students and researchers to make sure we had a note of all the Moslems. The head of the section is an old acquaintance of mine and we went out afterwards for a bite to eat not far from here. I warned him he'd probably have Hara to contend with before long."

Otani ignored his subordinate's irrepressible bounciness. "I've read the statements the people at the Arima police station took from the hotel staff over the weekend," he said. "Not very helpful. I think I'll go up there again myself tomorrow and look around a bit more." Kimura gave him a wary look as Otani spoke again. "Well, don't keep me in suspense. What have you found out that's making you look so pleased with yourself?"

Kimura shrugged. "Oh, nothing much. Beyond the fact that Abdalla doesn't seem to have had his mind on his research. Even making allowances for the fact that he hadn't been here long, he didn't show the slightest interest in getting down to work. In fact, the professor who was supposed to supervise him was so worried that he'd been on the phone to the Japan Society for the Promotion of Science in Tokyo to ask their advice. They were providing his travelling and subsistence funds."

Otani's eyes snapped brightly open. He now showed no signs of having put away a fair amount of sake during the previous couple of hours. Kimura beamed with satisfaction and unobtrusively plucked at his trouser-legs. It always distressed him to have to sit on tatami mats because of the disastrous effects on his expensive tailoring, but on this occasion it was well worth it to see the look on Otani's normally gravely inscrutable features.

"Very interesting." Otani reached out and poured another

51

healthy slug of whisky into Kimura's glass. "Tell me more."

"There isn't much to tell. He had one meeting with the professor after he arrived, but Abdalla was very vague about his research interests: hardly talked like a scientist at all apparently, in spite of his Ph.D. Said he needed a while to settle down, and hasn't been seen at the University since. Nor has he made much use of the study-bedroom they reserved for him at the University guest-house."

Kimura sipped his whisky appreciatively. "And there's something else. On Saturday we notified the deaths of both Abdalla and Fuhaid to their respective embassies in Tokyo through the Foreign Ministry Liaison Office in Osaka in accordance with the agreed procedures. The United Arab Emirates people reacted in a businesslike sort of way and have already been in touch with his employers to ask them to identify Fuhaid's body formally, then contact the Imam at the mosque and arrange a funeral. They're sending someone down to sort out his financial affairs, too." Otani nodded. He had every confidence in Kimura's ability to take care of such tiresome formalities.

Kimura leaned forward conspiratorially, glass in hand. "On the other hand, the Sudanese seem to be in a great state. An official flew from Tokyo and rushed straight to the mortuary on Saturday. Turned up there without notice while we were meeting in your office, actually. Migishima took an urgent phone call from the attendant and had to go over to witness the identification. He put it in his daily report but didn't think to mention it to me till this morning. Infuriating. By then this Sudanese diplomat had brought in an undertaker, had the body sealed in a lead-lined coffin and whisked it off to Osaka Airport to be flown home right away. Had a perfect right to, of course, but. . ."

Otani took a deep breath and drank some sake. "Not very clever of Migishima to leave it over the weekend, I agree. I wonder if he understood Japanese? Abdalla, I mean."

It seemed such an inconsequential question that Kimura looked quite startled. "I rather doubt it," he said. "I think

52

most Japanese scientists nowadays use English pretty freely, though. They have to be able to, with all their American contacts. And this man was sure to have been able to speak English."

"All very peculiar. Not much we can do about it tonight, though, is there?" Otani shifted restlessly on his zabuton and Kimura sensed that the appropriate moment to depart had arrived.

He scrambled to his stockinged feet as Hanae opened the sliding door to the room. "I must be going now. I'm very sorry to have disturbed you. Thank you very much for the whisky."

Making no attempt to detain him, Hanae and Otani followed their unexpected guest to the little entrance hall and watched as he inserted his feet into a pair of soft, expensive-looking shoes. "Very interesting," Otani murmured again almost to himself. "I'm very glad you looked in, Kimura. Goodnight, then."

After they had seen him off the Otanis returned to the living-room. "I think I might watch the television for a while," Otani said. Hanae looked at him with a small smile.

"All right," she said. "I'll go on up to bed." She was fairly sure he didn't hear a word she said.

Chapter VII

"Well, I intend to go anyway," Junko Migishima was saying at much the same time in a decided sort of way to her husband as she spread their bedding on the floor of the very small inner room of their flat a few miles away from the Otanis' house. It was a four-and-a-half mat room, about nine feet square. The living-room was only a little larger, six mats in size but Western-style, and in addition they had a tiny kitchen and a very small bathroom. The flat was in a new but featureless block, and they had taken out a huge loan to secure it. Friends were envious of the amount of space they had at their disposal, particularly with Junko a working police officer who didn't spend all that much time at home anyway.

Migishima himself was sitting in front of the television set in the living-room, having just switched it off with a sense of dutiful achievement after watching a programme on the educational channel about Democracy and The Media. He now sighed, stood up and pulled off his sweater. It was comparatively rare for them to be able to manage a quiet evening at home together, and he was sorry that Junko had chosen bed-time to revert to the subject of the local Moslem community. It had become a sensitive matter with him since earlier that day when Kimura had read his report and realised that the body of the Sudanese researcher had been spirited away from the mortuary attached to the municipal hospital over the weekend. Migishima was still unable to understand what he had done wrong, especially in view of the fact that Kimura was forever haranguing him on the importance of using his discretion and not bothering senior officers unnecessarily. It had not helped matters that Junko had obviously not shared his way of thinking about the episode.

"I can't see what you expect to get out of it," he now said grumpily. "And it'll be in your own free time. You know what Inspector Hara said. Besides, Kyoto's outside our jurisdiction." He moodily continued to undress, draping his clothes over the back of a chair. Although the Migishimas had comparatively few bulky possessions it was a nightmare to keep the place tidy, and they made no attempt to do so at night.

"If I choose to go to Kyoto at my own expense on my day off, that's nothing to do with Hara-san," Junko retorted, having taken off her own blouse and reaching behind her back to unclip her bra. Migishima eyed her small but pretty breasts hopefully until they disappeared from view in the cotton yukata she slipped into before removing the rest of her clothes. "I just wish you'd come and keep me company, that's all. You have a rest-day next Saturday too."

"I know," he said worriedly. "It's not that I *mind* going with you, Jun-chan. It's just that you said it's a sort of private meeting. In the first place, I don't see how we can just turn up without an invitation, and in the second place we'd be so conspicuous. They'd be bound to guess we're police officers."

Junko looked up at the hefty young man affectionately, went over to him and put her arms round him. Her head reached no higher than his upper chest and she nuzzled him there briefly before breaking away and skipping towards the bathroom. "I know The Heart-Throb teases you about looking like a policeman even in plain clothes," she said, "but I don't think you do. And I certainly don't think I do."

Migishima put on his own yukata and pottered about until the bathroom door opened and Junko emerged, looking about seventeen years old devoid of make-up. "Why are you so keen on going?" he demanded.

"Go and clean your teeth," Junko said, then followed him and continued talking through the open door while gazing at his large back. "You seem to have forgotten that I *am* still involved on the fringes of the rape case at the Kobe Women's Junior College. You remember. The girl who claimed to have been attacked by a prowler in the dormitory toilets."

"Orh hourhe I hihenha." Migishima rinsed, spat and tried again when no longer foaming at the mouth with toothpaste. "Of course I remember. You said you didn't believe her, but Inspector Hara took it seriously."

"Right. Don't forget I talked to her first. It took her a whole week to report the so-called incident to the Ikuta police station, and needless to say they don't have any women officers there." Junko interrupted herself with a delicate snort. "The don't have enough women police *anywhere*. Especially detectives." Migishima had heard her on this theme often enough before, and philosophically returned to his ablutions.

"I had my doubts about her right from the beginning, when I went back to the college with her and made her show me where it was supposed to have happened. I put in a very candid report to Hara-san, but he preferred to believe her story."

"I know. Our section was asked to supply him with a list of names of all the Moslem males in the area over the age of sixteen, with our file copies of the photos on their Alien Registration Cards. Inspector Kimura was furious."

"I dare say he was. Well, I saw the girl again today on Hara's instructions, to show her those self-same photos. At least he's sensible enough to let me handle her. I took her out

56

for a cup of coffee and got her talking. She really is the most incompetent liar I've come across for quite a time." Junko smiled reflectively. "The photo of the man concerned *was* among them, but it wasn't at all the way she said originally. After a while it all came out in a rush. She was quite relieved to unburden herself to another woman – not all that many years older than herself, when you come to think of it. The long and the short of it is that the silly girl has been having an affair with him, got pregnant and wanted to get an abortion while making everybody feel sorry for her."

"Oh." Migishima neatly replaced the towel he had been using, switched off the light and emerged from the bathroom, and together they made their way to bed. It was far from completely dark in the little room even with all the lights out. The window was concealed by a wooden lattice-work and paper shoji screen which softened the harsh mercury lighting of the high-speed toll-road which was located not more than a hundred metres or so away from the apartment block; but the developers had not seen fit to install double glazing, and the sound of traffic permeated the lives of all the residents twenty-four hours a day. All the same, the young Migishimas took conscious pride in their home and fiercely enjoyed entering every night the modest capsule of privacy represented by their bedroom. Migishima put a big arm round her shoulders as Junko continued her story.

"The boy she's been sleeping with is – well, hardly a boy really, a graduate student at Kobe University. And he's from Indonesia. She got into conversation with him originally in a coffee shop not far from the college – or from the mosque, of course. Then he invited her to a meeting of this KISS organisation, the Kinki International Students' Society, and she joined."

Migishima raised himself up on his elbow and tentatively inserted his free hand in the front of Junko's yukata, happy to encounter no resistance on her part. "I still don't know why you want to go to the next meeting in Kyoto."

"I'm just curious, that's all. I decided there was no point in causing trouble for the girl. I told her I'd report back that she couldn't identify anyone from the photos, that the file would be marked 'Assailant Unknown' and that she could go off and have her abortion without any fuss. She was so grateful when I promised not to let her parents know the truth that she told me quite a lot about her boyfriend and what he'd told *her* about the Islamic community here. And she invited me to the next KISS meeting as her guest."

Migishima was so taken aback that he withdrew his hand, which Junko quickly grasped and firmly replaced on her breast. "You mean she's going to go on meeting the Indonesian?"

"Oh, yes. She thinks he's wonderful. She doesn't want a baby by him, though."

"I can well believe it." Emboldened by the drift of the discussion, Migishima lowered his head and whispered into his wife's ear. "When are you going to stop taking the pill, Jun-chan?"

It wasn't so much that Migishima wanted a child as that his mother nagged him so about the matter whenever he made one of his duty phone calls to her, and Junko knew this perfectly well. "Have you been phoning the Nada house again? Really, Ken'ichi! We've been over all that quite often enough."

Without any warning Junko then scrambled on top of him and stripped off her yukata. "Want a fight?" Her tone of simulated menace both amused and excited him and Migishima nodded, speechless as she seized his wrists and tried to force them down at either side of his head. In fact Junko was an advanced student of the *aikido* art of unarmed combat, and for all her diminutive size could have given a very good account of herself in a serious bout with Migishima. However, they both knew what would begin to happen within less than a minute of their starting to tussle with each other, and it did.

Chapter VIII

"No, Mr Khan," Kimura said firmly. "I must make it clear to you that I am not myself interested at all in buying any carpets."

The naturally liquid eyes of Abdul Ghafoor Khan took on a woebegone expression, as though they were about to brim over with actual tears. "Very keen prices, sir," he muttered. "Top-hole merchandise, as supplied to ambassadors and members of the European royalty." Then he brightened and extended slender brown fingers to Kimura's lapel, which he fondled delicately. "Tailoring, sir!" he cried eagerly. "You are a natty dresser, that I can see. From three hundred swatches of finest worsted – your free choice, and we can deliver to you in ten days. A three-piece suit for eighty thousand yen, tailored to perfection . . ."

In spite of himself Kimura was drawn. "Really? Eighty thousand?"

"Oh my goodness yes. Or two for one hundred and fifty thousand. Latest styles from Milan, Paris, London, you just

59

tear the page out of whatever magazine you see them in and our expert cutters do the rest . . ." Kimura cleared his throat noisily. "Yes, well, Mr Khan, perhaps later. Perhaps I *might* take a look at your material samples, but just now I must remind you that I am a police officer, and I should be grateful if you would answer a few questions."

"Indeed indeed indeed. I am all ears, you know." Abdul Ghafoor Khan sat back in his chair importantly, but Kimura had an uneasy feeling that he did so in order the more easily to size him up for the new suit or suits which the Pakistani was certainly going to sell him sooner or later, and cursed himself for giving the man even a word of encouragement. They were sitting in the lobby of the Oriental Hotel, which has a sort of lounge-terrace at the back where light refreshments are served. When Kimura had telephoned the Pakistani trader at his home number he had proposed to call at the Khan residence, but his suggestion had been firmly rejected. So had his alternative invitation to Mr Khan to drop in and see him at Hyogo prefectural police headquarters. In the circumstances Kimura felt no compunction about accepting the cup of coffee and slab of creamy cheesecake which were now reposing on the table between them.

"It was good of you to spare the time to meet me here, Mr Khan." Kimura had had no trouble in recognising him on arrival in the lobby. Khan had said over the phone that he would be wearing a checked sports jacket, and the garment he wore over what, from the tiny alligator device on the left breast, Kimura recognised to be a Lacoste sports shirt of primrose yellow was indeed in a striking combination of brown and yellow checks. Kimura surreptitiously studied it as they sat there, wondering whether it was the handiwork of the same "expert cutters" who would provide him with a bespoke suit for eighty thousand, or roughly a week's basic pay.

"Would you prefer to speak Japanese?" Khan asked in that language.

Kimura was not surprised by the implication that he had a good command of it, since he knew from his files that Khan

60

had lived in Kobe for the past fifteen years, but shook his head. "Thank you, but English will be fine," he replied, then sat back for a moment to marshal his thoughts before beginning.

"Now, when we first met a few minutes ago, I explained that I am not concerned with your business affairs – "

"All in tip-top order, Inspector. Tax, Alien Registration – I am keeping my nose damned clean."

"I know, I know," Kimura said soothingly. He did, having had Abdul Ghafoor Khan thoroughly checked out with the relevant authorities before setting up the appointment. "I don't want to ask you about yourself. I want to know if you can tell me anything about Hossein Fuhaid."

Khan ladled an astonishing quantity of sugar into his coffee and stirred it vigorously. "Poor Fuhaid. What a rotten show. You know, that man was a perfect size thirty-six? We could have fitted him to a T straight off the peg, but of course all our merchandise is to measure, you know." He pulled himself together hastily. "Apologies, Inspector. But Fuhaid was a good customer and friend of mine."

"I understand. You met him through your connection with the mosque here, is that right?" Khan hesitated briefly, then nodded as he leaned forward and picked up his coffee cup. Kimura noticed with some interest that the skin of his hand and wrist was almost exactly the same colour as the liquid within the cup.

"At the mosque, that is so. Hossein Fuhaid came here – good gracious, it must be three years ago. Sought us out, my good sir. Turned up at Friday prayers one week and then as regular as clockwork after that. Not easy, you know, for a man working in a Japanese company to get time off for prayers. Extended lunch hour, I expect he called it."

"And you're a member of the mosque committee, I understand, Mr Khan. But Fuhaid was an Arab, from the United Arab Emirates."

The large eyes all at once looked less gentle. "My brother in Allah, Mr Kimura. You might not understand that."

61

Kimura was taken aback by the sudden chilling of the atmosphere. "Of course, of course," he said in a mollifying tone. "I'm quite sure you extend a very warm welcome to all new members of your congregation, regardless of nationality."

"We do." The words seemed to hang in the air between them, and Kimura conveyed a forkful of cheesecake to his mouth while working out how to proceed: it was delicious.

"Well, you must have been greatly shocked by the news of Mr Fuhaid's death. Not to mention that of Dr el Abdalla a few hours earlier."

"Abdalla too, yes. You should crack down on that sort of reckless driving, you know, Inspector. All these young fellows allowed to tear about the place on their motorbikes —"

"It was a taxi, Mr Khan. Unfortunately nobody managed to get its number."

Khan shook his head from side to side as he sucked in air through his teeth. "I know. I saw the whole thing. Both shocking affairs. Abdalla, you see — well, we hardly knew him, but poor Fuhaid was much respected. An example to us all of true Islamic zeal. To take his own life like that . . . so unnecessary." The disappearance of Abdul Ghafoor Khan's earlier slightly comic accent and manner was evident to Kimura, who became abruptly aware that the Pakistani was probably a lot harder and shrewder than he had initially allowed himself to suppose.

"Yes, he did . . . die, Mr Khan. And it is my duty and that of my colleagues to try to find out why. No suicide note has been found either at the hotel where he died or at his apartment, and enquiries at his place of work have not produced any evidence that he had any particular worries. Fuhaid was divorced. Can you tell me anything about his private life here in Kobe?"

"How do you know he was divorced?" Khan's face had become hard and his manner sharply challenging.

Kimura sighed. "Because he stated as much when applying

for his Alien Registration, Mr Khan. There is nothing secret about it." He looked up into Khan's face suddenly. "I take it that you were aware of the fact?"

Khan gestured dismissively with one hand. "Yes, yes, of course. It is no shame in Islamic society."

"A man of forty-three. Middle-aged, but no more. Might he have become involved with a woman here? A Japanese woman? Or perhaps even someone from within your community?"

Now the dark pools of Khan's eyes seemed to ice over, and Kimura revised his assessment of the Pakistani's character even more radically. "You obviously know very little about Islam, Mr Kimura. We take good care of our womenfolk, you know. Protect them."

"But all the same divorce is no shame?" Kimura was nettled by Khan's new, hard attitude and wanted to tax him further with the illogicality of what he had said, but something held him back.

Khan ignored the interruption. "Hossein was a good man. A religious man. I am confident that his private life was very orderly."

Kimura changed direction. "I understand that you yourself were born in Rawalpindi, Mr Khan. You have your wife and children here with you, of course, but do you still have family connections in Pakistan?" He half expected Khan to react with outrage to personal questions, and was pleasantly surprised when instead the thin brown face creased into a broad smile.

"What a question to ask a Pakistani! From a Japanese too! Oh my good sir, you think you people have strong family connections – you are not holding a candle to us, let me tell you." A bony hand rested briefly on Kimura's knee, and Khan lowered his voice confidentially. "How do you think I am offering genuine Afghan carpets at such keen prices? Fine brass-ware too, even though this merchandise is not moving so well these days? Rawalpindi is very much the right place to have brothers, cousins, nephews and friends etcetera just now."

"Did you have any sort of business dealings with Fuhaid, Mr Khan? I mean, with the shipping agency he worked for?"

"No connection there at all, Inspector. He was on the export side, you see. I told you already, he was a good customer of mine as well as my friend. *Always* bought his suits from the tailoring firm I am associated with. Here, take this card."

Like a conjuror Abdul Ghafoor Khan suddenly tweaked a printed card from an inner pocket and thrust it at Kimura. It was larger than a standard Japanese name-card and rather amateurishly produced. Kimura studied the message printed on it:

KOBE'S PREMIER GENTS OUTFITTER!
Serving the Cosmopolitan Community

MOHAMMED KHAN BROS.
"Our Fit is Our Pride"
Also associated with

PESHAWAR PAKISTANI RESTAURANT – "It's a Feast!"

A cluster of telephone numbers and addresses in fine print at the bottom was supplemented by a printed map on the reverse of the card, indicating the locations of the various enterprises with which the brothers Khan were involved.

Kimura stowed the card away in his pocket. "We're not getting on very fast, Mr Khan," he said tersely. "Can't you give me *any* reason why Fuhaid may have taken his own life?"

The second comic interlude was over, and Khan's eyelids drooped, giving him a slightly sinister appearance. "An unnecessary death," was all he said again, before falling silent.

"All right. Let's go back to Dr el Abdalla for a moment. You saw the incident in which he was killed – in fact you assisted the police by identifying him."

The eyelids snapped open. "I did. A terrible accident. I

64

cannot pretend that Abdalla was a popular member of our community, though."

"Really? You said a little while ago that you hardly knew him. Wasn't he as welcome as any other newly arrived Moslem?"

Khan looked at his watch. "I must be getting along, Inspector," he said abruptly. "I suggest that you should ask someone else's opinion of Dr el Abdalla."

He rose to his feet and Kimura followed suit in some surprise. "Very well, I won't keep you. I may need to get in touch with you again, though, Mr Khan."

Abdul Ghafoor Khan bent, picked up the bill which the waitress had left when she brought their refreshments, and marched off with it to the cashier's desk as Kimura trailed in his wake. After paying, the slender Pakistani moved purposefully towards the glass doors at the main exit to the hotel. Kimura followed, but it was not until they were both outside the building that Khan looked at him again. Then he stopped short and tapped Kimura delicately on the chest. "Quite candidly, Inspector, Abdalla was a pushy, obnoxious sort of fellow." After a short pause, he reverted to his original style. "Now remember, my good sir, and tell your host of friends. The finest cut and finish, sacrifice prices and your money returned if not delighted! Five minutes walk from here!"

Then he was gone, a gaudy figure among the soberly-dressed passers-by, and it was a full minute before Kimura unlocked his umbrella from the rack and set off in the rain to walk the even shorter distance back to headquarters.

Chapter IX

In Kobe, the rain in which a multi-coloured crop of umbrellas mushroomed amounted to little more than a shower, but there was a torrential downpour in Arima as Otani emerged from the Grand View Hotel. He stood indecisively for a few moments in the shelter of the entrance, regretting the self-inflicted necessity to take the train or bus rather than be driven back to Kobe in comfort in his official Toyota Police Special by the devoted Tomita.

Tomita had earnestly advised against Otani's idea not only during the drive up but again when setting him down at the hotel an hour and a half previously. Otani had perversely sent him away all the same, rather looking forward to the prospect of being out of touch for a few hours, an anonymous man in his late fifties using public transport as the great majority of Japanese still do, even in an age when the English expression "my car" has become part of their own language. The Otanis had never owned a car of their own and on their private outings managed perfectly well without one.

Otani sniffed the damp air, reflected that a little rain never hurt anybody, and prepared to make a dash for the bus stop two or three hundred yards away; but then noticed plastic umbrellas on sale at a souvenir shop just across the street under a large sign announcing their price. Reflecting that even a cup of coffee would cost more than the two hundred yen they were asking, he sprinted across the road instead and looked at them. The frames were white, and the choice of translucent polythene covers seemed to be between orange, green and purple, the colours of cheap boiled sweets.

"Haven't you got any plain ones? You know, no colour," Otani enquired of the ancient woman who shuffled forward from the recesses of the shop to serve him, knocking over a puffy blown-up model of a Boeing 747 in the livery of All Nippon Airlines as she did so. The stopper came out and they both watched it shrivel into a wrinkled little heap, like the sloughed skin of a snake.

"My son will blow it up again," she said. "I haven't got the puff these days. Have you?" She rummaged through the umbrellas still muttering to herself until Otani stopped her.

"It's all right, Granny, I'll have a purple one." He was not particularly put off by the prospect of using one of the gaudy ones and indeed the proper salaryman's umbrella he currently most commonly used from the small collection which had accumulated at the house over the years was a rather pleasing dull green.

It took some time to conclude the transaction, since the old lady was disposed to chat for a while about the old days, and Otani was quite willing to indulge her. It was in any case quite interesting to learn that she had a grand-daughter in the Takarazuka All-Girl Revue company, and her rambling remarks stuck in his mind as he eventually headed for the bus-stop in the lurid gloom cast over him by his new umbrella. Takarazuka was no further away from home than Arima itself, yet he and Hanae hadn't been there to see a show since their daughter Akiko had been a little girl in the nineteen-fifties.

As he bent to peer at the timetable posted near the bus-stop Otani wondered if the current production was as glamorous as the one that had made Akiko-chan's eyes look like saucers nearly thirty years before. The town of Takarazuka was, of course, no more than a few miles away from Arima, and there was even a bus going there in, let's see, six minutes' time. Whereas the next one down to Kobe wasn't due for another twenty-five minutes.

Otani changed his mind several times as he stood there, but when the Takarazuka bus sloshed to a halt beside him and the automatic door hissed open he boarded it without hesitation, a distinctly gleeful sense of wickedness possessing him and remaining somewhere in the background of his consciousness as the bus swayed and jolted along the narrow mountain roads. Certainly he felt as if he deserved a treat after his frustrating conversations at the hotel.

The manageress had been effusively helpful without really adding anything to what she had divulged during his first interview with her on the evening of the party and the discovery of Fuhaid's body. More irritating was the fact that the girl receptionist who had checked him in, and been on duty again in the early afternoon when the Arab and his female companion must have gone out, was having a rest-day: Otani wanted to talk to her himself. There was no help to be had from the young woman who ran the souvenir stall in the lobby, a pert creature who sniffily explained that she wasn't in the habit of watching ladies go to and from the toilet, or gentlemen either for that matter.

Otani had been shown the room again, and looked thoughtfully at the sunken bath in which Fuhaid had died. The room next door was very obviously occupied, and by a strenuously enthusiastic couple, to judge by the thumping noises and female moans of rapture clearly audible through the adjoining wall.

The report drawn up by the local Arima police included a statement by the room maid that the sheets had borne evidence of earlier lovemaking, and having now had a word with her Otani was quite willing to be guided by her experienced judgment. All the same, he was glad that Noguchi had been there after the removal of the body when she arrived to change them and had made her bundle them into a plastic laundry bag. They were now at the regional forensic laboratory, along with Fuhaid's clothes and the "Handinife" found when the blood-red water was drained away.

No member of the staff of the hotel could recall seeing the mystery woman leave the premises: Otani was disappointed but not greatly surprised. Thanks to the general tightening up and enforcement of fire regulations following some horrifying incidents involving much loss of life at Japanese resort hotels in recent years, and the gutting of the huge Hotel New Japan in Tokyo, emergency exits were now usually unobstructed and capable of being opened easily from within. There was such a door at the end of the corridor no more than a few yards away, and on opening it Otani had seen how easily anyone could slip out of the building and through the service gate, especially under cover of darkness.

The ten-kilometre ride to Takarazuka took only about twenty minutes. It was still raining when Otani got off the bus, but not nearly so heavily, and there were a few breaks in the clouds to the west. As in the case of Arima, new buildings had sprouted all over Takarazuka since Otani's last visit, but there was no mistaking the approach to the so-called "Takarazuka Family Land", the amusement park across the river in which the Grand Theatre is situated.

Otani headed for the bridge and was soon crossing it and looking at the stretch to his left which had been dammed to produce a boating lake, also, needless to say, part of the Takarazuka entertainment complex. The theatre itself was visible from the bridge, looking from the outside like a modern hypermarket of the kind that are beginning to spring up all over Japan. Streamers on the approach road celebrated the 70th anniversary of the founding of the All-Girls' Opera Company, as it was originally called by the railway tycoon who developed the private Hankyu Line which still controls the modern conglomerate.

Otani picked his way gravely among the little groups of visitors standing about outside the gates to the Grand Theatre. He was in luck: the matinée performance was due to start in twenty minutes, and there were middle-priced seats available, so he bought one and entered a world of fantasy, like a royal ballroom in a Walt Disney cartoon feature.

The lobby was enormous; perfumed and softly draped, with elaborate chandeliers high above and photographs of Takarazuka stars lining the walls. With his long sight Otani was able to make out the names attached to faces he saw every day in advertisements on television, in newspapers and in every Hankyu Line train and station. Among the male role players there was Mayuka Go, smouldering like a young delinquent, full-lipped Noeru Misa and sullen Machika Seri, while the femmes who took his eye were bitchy-looking Chihiro Arata, the deliciously gamine Hitomi Harukaze and tremblingly vulnerable Hitomi Kuroki. Otani regretted that he had not thought to ask the old lady in the souvenir shop the name of her grand-daughter: it was odd to think that she might conceivably be one of these.

The great majority of the patrons milling their way about the foyer with its boutiques selling records and cassettes of previous productions, photographs and programmes, fluffy toys, handbags and trashy souvenirs, or emerging from the restaurants and snack bars to make their way to the auditorium, were women of every age. Many were respectably turned-out young mothers with their daughters, but there were also many old ladies and girls in their late teens or early twenties in couples and groups. Otani gaped at one plump young woman wearing a tight sweater and shiny gold pants like running shorts over black tights and high-heeled shoes; then turned aside in some haste lest he should be taken for one of the sly old male voyeurs who were also dotted about the foyer.

There were quite a few foreigners exclaiming to each other

in loud voices. Otani supposed they must be tourists, but wondered a little about one, a woman in her late twenties with striking red hair. She was talking with what seemed like anxious urgency to a Japanese woman in a well-cut trouser suit: her companion was obviously some years older than herself. Something about the older woman's style and manner suggested to Otani that she belonged there at Takarazuka, and he was not greatly surprised when she and the foreigner passed through the barrier to the auditorium without presenting any tickets but to the accompaniment of respectful bows from the attendants, both male and female.

Then Otani went to his own seat, and as soon as the curtain rose forgot all about red-headed foreigners, dead Arabs and everything else except the spectacle on the stage. The company's seventieth anniversary revue was called in English *Takarazuka Forever!* and fell into two parts, the first of which was a tale of love, tragedy and buffoonery in seventeenth-century Tokyo, or Edo as it was then known. Otani became rather confused by the plot, but smiled indulgently at the women dressed as samurai, swaggering about the stage in splendidly arrogant fashion, going in for some creditable sword-play and snarling at each other in menacing contralto voices. The acting was lively, tidy and not without real humour, and he enjoyed it, but during the interval felt slightly ashamed of himself for wasting official time and nearly decided to head back to Kobe.

Something held him back, though, and he returned to his seat for the second half and the revue proper, telling himself that he would slip out quietly after ten minutes or so; but he lost all sense of time when the orchestra struck up and the curtain rose again, for a splendid production number involving at least eighty to ninety girls on the huge stage. Otani gazed in simple pleasure at the chorus in a froth of feathers, plumes and suspenders, the male role stars in front in sequinned trousers and tail-coats, and everyone singing and dancing with an uninhibited gaiety which made him feel distinctly elated.

71

Scene followed scene at two- or three-minute intervals, with innumerable costume changes displaying the work of a zanily imaginative designer. There were pastoral scenes with girls in Kate Greenaway pretties, bows in their hair and attendant "young men" in striped blazers and white ducks, doffing their straw boaters to reveal brilliantined hair parted in the middle. There was a Spanish-style spectacular, all castanets and mantillas, and a sentimental scene set outside a Paris theatre complete with a complement of drawling stage-door Johnnies in white tie and tails.

Otani recognised many of the tunes, although he didn't know the names of such evergreens as "A Pretty Girl is Like a Melody" or "It Was Just One of Those Things", but he had a fine time, stayed till the very end and sauntered out humming to himself in high good humour, unaware that the red-haired foreigner was a few yards behind him, also making for the station.

Chapter X

"I'm home!" Otani called out cheerfully as he rattled open the sliding outer door of his house, noting as he did that the small clump of bamboo in the narrow space between the front of the house and the wall which surrounded it needed tidying up. Many of the younger generation seemed to disregard the formerly universal custom of ensuring that every house had its pine and plum trees and stand of bamboo to guarantee health and prosperity; but even the arch-traditionalist Otani accepted that it was difficult to observe it if one happened to live in an apartment block. Nevertheless, he was personally soothed by an awareness of the presence of their own "pine-bamboo-plum" symbols, planted there before he had been born by his father, the stern and upright Professor Otani of Osaka University, who in his old age had so deplored his only son's choice of profession.

"Welcome home!" Hanae's response was as immediate as always, but Otani noticed something odd about the sound of her voice, and soon understood the reason when he saw an alien pair of shoes neatly arranged by the polished wooden step up into the house. They were a woman's, with higher heels than Hanae customarily wore with Western dress. A visitor. It struck Otani that they seemed to be having altogether too many of these lately, and he frowned as he deposited his new purple plastic umbrella in the stand, slipped off his own shoes and stepped up and into the downstairs room.

There he was greeted by the sight of the tops of two female heads as both his wife and her younger sister Michiko bowed in welcome to him. In some haste Otani sank to his knees and returned the compliment, then sat back and regarded his sister-in-law. "Well, Michiko-san!" he said as affably as he could manage. "What a pleasant surprise. I haven't seen you for a very long time. I hope you're keeping well?"

"Thanks to you, yes," Michiko replied formally. The exchange was really just a string of sounds to both of them, though Otani would have been the first to laugh had he thought about the literal meaning of her reply, which was in fact, "In your honourable shadow, I flourish." In fact he had very little in common with Michiko. He did not actively dislike her but found her airs and graces somewhat trying, and therefore usually contrived to be out of the house when he knew she was to pay one of her rare sisterly calls on Hanae.

Michiko had just turned forty, and in Otani's strictly private opinion was too strenuously protracting her dogged battle against the advancing years. Other Japanese women he encountered generally assumed with every appearance of active enthusiasm whatever role society allotted to them. Thus, an office lady was an office lady, invariably bright, charming and deferential. A tour bus guide was equally bright and charming, but was additionally a fountain of information about places on the route (whether of interest or not), as well as a dedicated and authoritative rounder-up of stray passengers who showed any subversive inclination to leave the proximity of the flag on its little pole in her upraised, white-gloved hand.

74

Married ladies were – well, married ladies. Especially when pregnant, it being quite the thing to go into low heels, socks and loose smock dresses within a few weeks, if not days, after conception. Above all, academic spinsters were supposed to dress modestly, have glasses, wear their hair drawn severely back, and eschew make-up.

Michiko flouted these well-established conventions. Although an assistant professor of History at the famous Doshisha Women's University in Kyoto, she had undergone a late flowering and assumed in recent years an image which to Otani was an unfortunate combination of unsuitable trendiness and liberated outspokenness. He suspected that she had only with reluctance followed her elder sister's example in bowing to him in greeting, and tried not to look too obviously at his sister-in-law's extraordinary hair as Hanae poured him out a cup of green tea and passed him a small but expensive-looking bean-jam cake.

Michiko looked to Otani somewhat like his idea of a Russian peasant. She was wearing a loose, vaguely ethnic blouse belted at the waist over baggy trousers. The hair which alarmed Otani was a mass of tight, springy curls, and she was made up with great boldness, her purplish lipstick reminding him of the young tarts he occasionally saw hanging about the vicinity of bars and discos in Kobe. He could remember quite well when Michiko had looked the part of the earnest young academic, and the transformation distressed him.

"You look very . . . lively, Michiko-san," he said experimentally. "I see you're not wearing glasses any more."

"Contact lenses." Michiko spoke in a businesslike way.

Hanae intervened. "Try the cake," she urged her husband. "Mi-chan brought them specially from Kyoto for us. From the famous shop near the Hyakumanben crossing."

"I don't normally eat that kind of old-fashioned cake," Michiko added scornfully. "Bad for the figure. I keep telling my students the same thing, but they won't listen. You're home early." Michiko invariably addressed Hanae as *Ne-chan* or "Elder Sister" as she had from childhood, and for a number of years after Hanae married Otani had used courteous forms of speech to him. It would have been unthinkable for her to use his given name, Tetsuo, which even Hanae seldom uttered, generally addressing her husband by the most affectionate of the several words for "you". Nowadays Michiko avoided calling Otani anything at all, which gave her conversation a rather masculine bluntness that made Hanae wince inside.

"Only half an hour or so," Otani protested gently. "I've been . . . out, and I came straight home instead of going back to the office first." For a moment he was tempted to shock both Michiko and Hanae by telling them that he had been to Takarazuka to look at the girls' legs, but decided he would save the story for Hanae alone, later. "What brings you to Rokko?"

"I had to go to a meeting this afternoon at Kobe University. It's so near that I rang Ne-chan to see if she was at home, and dropped in for a chat. I must be going soon though." Otani was relieved to hear it, having glumly supposed they would have to invite her to share their evening meal. "Some conference of historians?" he suggested, merely in order to make conversation.

"Mi-chan's had another paper published in the *Journal of Modern Historical Studies*," Hanae put in equably. "On the role of women in postwar Japanese politics."

Otani did not intend to be rude. "Oh. Have they had one?" he enquired.

Michiko gave him a withering look. "Have you two or three hours to spare? Or perhaps you ought to join my seminar at the university." She pursed her empurpled lips and looked all of forty in her irritation. "To answer your *other* question, though, it wasn't an academic conference that brought me to Kobe University. It was a meeting of the Advisory Board of KISS."

"Of what?" Although Otani knew no English, he was familiar enough with the word "kiss" which had become a Japanese verb since the war, and with the same meaning.

Michiko smiled in a slightly arch way. "A good play on words, don't you think? It's actually the initial letters of the real English name of the organisation – the Kinki International Students' Society. 'Kiss' implies warm friendship, after all, and that's the objective of the society, to promote international friendship."

Otani hated being lectured at, and in any case found it difficult to follow the drift of Michiko's remarks. "If it's a student society, what are you doing in it?" He did not notice the quiver of Hanae's lips as she suppressed a smile: she had been wondering the same thing.

Michiko ran a hand with care through her oddly permed hair. "I'm not *in* it. I'm a member of the Advisory Board," she said in an exasperated way. "The regular members are students from any of the universities in the whole Kinki area. There's a strict balance in numbers between Japanese and foreign students, though, so obviously membership is much more difficult to obtain for Japanese. The Advisory Board screens applications from Japanese students to join. There are twelve of us . . ." she paused briefly before continuing " . . . younger and more active teachers on the Board, representing the important universities in the area."

Even Hanae was moved to comment. "I'm rather surprised that the regular members don't object to an arrangement like that. I should have thought they'd prefer to decide for themselves which new members to admit."

Michiko sniffed as she took another of the cakes she affected to despise. "I'm sure they welcome our advice," she said. "Besides, they use university premises for their meetings, and that wouldn't be acceptable to the various authorities unless something like our Advisory Board existed."

Otani was already extremely bored and wished Michiko would go away so that he could have his evening bath and tell Hanae about Takarazuka over their meal, then settle down and watch television for a while. "Well, I hope you had a satisfactory meeting," he said heavily, stealing a glance at his watch.

"Not too bad, I suppose," Michiko allowed with a sigh. "It was particularly important for me today because the next regular meeting is at my college, on Saturday. We've all been a bit anxious because of a certain amount of bad feeling that's arisen between a group of Arab students and some who are Jewish. Then the Iranians don't exactly help matters, I must say."

Michiko rubbed her temples delicately, implying her weary acceptance of burdens of the order shouldered by the Secretary-General of the United Nations, but Otani wasn't looking. "Many Arab students, are there?" he demanded abruptly, and Michiko opened her eyes and blinked.

"What? Oh. No, not very many. Quite enough to be something of a nuisance, though." She began to make movements signalling her imminent departure. "I really must be going."

Hanae was astounded when her husband reached out a hand to detain Michiko. "You say it's hard for Japanese students to join, but presumably any foreigner is automatically entitled to membership. Would you say that in practice most of them take part? What about more senior people – researchers? Would they be likely to join? Do they get a pretty big turn-out at their meetings?"

Michiko looked at her brother-in-law in some surprise. "You seem very interested all of a sudden. Why don't you come and see for yourself on Saturday? You and Ne-chan would be very welcome to come as my guests. Needless to say members of the Advisory Board are all honorary members of KISS itself." She detached her arm from Otani's grasp and stood up. "To answer your questions, I would say that the great majority of foreign students in this area join KISS. Nearly all of them are postgraduate researchers anyway, and there's no age limit. Usually we expect to see about fifteen to twenty of them at regular meetings, but we're expecting a lot more on Saturday. The Jewish group have called for a special business meeting, you see."

Otani managed to go through the motions of bidding

Michiko a cordial farewell, but did not accompany her and Hanae to the door. He knew from experience that they would spend at least another ten minutes or more talking before Michiko finally wrenched herself away, and he spent the time in the small kitchen, trying to guess what they would be having for their evening meal. He had concluded that it was to be jumbo shrimp and was wondering whether Hanae might perhaps cook them in ginger when she appeared at his side and firmly closed the refrigerator door.

"Would you really like to go to this meeting of Mi-chan's on Saturday? She was very surprised that you seemed to be so interested. She made a point just now of stressing that her invitation was quite genuine."

"Oh, I'll think about it, but I doubt if it would be very interesting. . .it was just something of a coincidence when she started to talk about Arabs. Suddenly I seem to be surrounded by Moslems on every side. By the way, what's the matter with her hair? I didn't like to say anything."

Hanae smiled as she shook her head in affectionate despair. "There's nothing the matter with it. It's the *fashion*. Go and have your bath while I start the supper."

Otani dawdled in the doorway. "Shrimp, is it? Are you going to do them with ginger?"

"Wait and see." Hanae took her apron from its hook at the side of the store cupboard and turned her back decisively on her husband, who lingered a moment longer and then disappeared. When she next heard his voice Hanae decided that he must be at least half-way up the stairs.

"Well, I think it makes her look ridiculous. And those baggy trousers. Like those awful civilian uniform things women were supposed to wear during the war . . ."

Chapter XI

"If you have any idea what he's up to you know more than I do," Kimura said rather bitterly. "He went up to Arima again yesterday morning and didn't show up here for the rest of the day. I don't see what could have taken him so long." He leant back in his chair, stretched and yawned. "I really must get more sleep."

"He came in this morning for a while," Noguchi rumbled from where he was standing at the open door. "Then he had to go to see the Governor about – oh, it's you, Hara." He shifted his position to get a better view into the corridor. "Come in here a minute. Want to talk to you. Sit down over there." Kimura was rendered temporarily speechless with outrage as Noguchi beckoned Inspector Hara into *his* office and indicated the chair set aside for the use of *his* visitors. Rather uncertainly, Hara folded his pear-shaped body into a sitting position as instructed and blinked at Kimura. Noguchi remained standing in the doorway.

"Good afternoon, Inspector," Hara said to the glowering

Kimura. "I was just on my way to Records Section, but if there is anything I can do for you. . ."

"Need to get our heads together," Noguchi said. "Spoken to the Commander lately?" Noguchi's manner of speech was habitually crude and direct, but he almost always referred to Otani in his absence correctly and by title, unlike Kimura to whom he was "the Old Man", "the Chief" or sometimes "the Boss", even though the last of these words, used in English, was the usual designation bestowed on top gangsters.

"Yes. On the telephone this morning. He said he was about to go out, but we had a few words." A hint of smugness crept into Hara's expression as it appeared to dawn on him that he had stolen a march on the others.

"It's too bad!" The dam broke and the words burst out of Kimura. "He lectures us about working together and then does that kind of thing!"

"For your added information, Inspector, it was I who rang the Commander, not the other way round."

"You rang him? What for?"

"Calm down, Kimura. Why shouldn't he?" Noguchi had not moved, but somehow had taken on a slightly menacing air.

"I have no objection to describing the substance of our brief conversation," Hara added hastily, looking from one to the other of his two inexplicably irate colleagues. "I felt it incumbent upon me to advise the Commander that certain information has come into our possession as a result of the careful questioning of the neighbours of the late Hossein Fuhaid and also of his immediate colleagues at the shipping office at which he was employed. I know that many older police officers regret the breaking up of the old neighbourhood supervision groups which used to exercise quasi-legal functions up to and during the war, but I am bound to say that during my own admittedly comparatively brief career – "

"Hara. What on earth are you babbling about?" Kimura had sufficiently recovered himself to assume an exaggerated expression of bewilderment.

Hara took a breath and carried on remorselessly. "As I was

81

about to say, during my own career it has almost invariably been my experience that in any neighbourhood it is possible to find some elderly person, usually though not always a woman, who has little to do all day except watch people come and go and speculate about their business."

"Right." Gratified by Noguchi's terse endorsement of his words, Hara took off his glasses and polished them vigorously with a spotless white handkerchief. "Don't see many of those about," Noguchi added. "Handkerchiefs. It's all paper this and paper that nowadays."

"Look," Kimura said with heavy patience. "I hate to interrupt you two, but some of us have got work to do. So you got hold of some old girl who told you all the dirt on Fuhaid, did you? Well, what about sharing it with us?"

"It was in fact Woman Detective Officer Migishima who gained the confidence of an elderly lady who lives opposite the small block of luxury apartments in which Fuhaid lived. She has, it would appear, a deep-seated, ah, *mistrust* of foreigners, and seemed to be neither distressed nor surprised to hear of Fuhaid's death. She confided to Officer Migishima that she had long been of the opinion that he would come to no good."

A rumbling gurgle could be heard from the region of Noguchi's imposing belly and he shifted his position slightly as both the others turned their heads in his direction. "Missed lunch," he said blandly, and crossed his arms. "Go on, Hara." Hara blinked several times and consulted a small notebook he whisked from an inner pocket before continuing.

"Fuhaid did only the most basic shopping in the neighbourhood, it seems, at weekends. A few vegetables, bread, coffee, instant noodles, detergent and the like. On weekdays he left his flat each morning at about seven-thirty, and rarely arrived back before nine or ten at night."

"Yes, yes, all very predictable. Exactly what you would expect of a man living alone. Nothing very interesting there," Kimura said scornfully. "I live alone myself, have a very similar routine."

"You married, Hara?" It was Noguchi, an enquiring look on his battered face.

"Really, Ninja! That's hardly relevant, I should have – "

"Yes. Yes, I am." Hara had stopped twitching and a smile of singular tenderness spread over his face.

"Any kids?"

"One daughter. She's five. . .and another on the way."

"Ah."

Exasperated, Kimura spread his hands and arms in an extravagant gesture. "*Please!*" Then he lowered his voice to a dramatic whisper. "I beg of you, Hara. Will you *please* tell me what this old lady told Migishima's wife which is in the least interesting or conceivably relevant to our enquiries? Or what, if anything, has come out of the interviewing of the staff at the place where Fuhaid worked? For heaven's sake, over twenty thousand people commit suicide in Japan every year. All right. Fuhaid was a foreigner, so there's more paperwork involved. But this is getting ridiculous."

Hara resumed his trying official manner. "It would appear that Fuhaid entertained visitors at weekends and sometimes late at night. She identified the Pakistani Abdul Ghafoor Khan as a frequent caller over a long period, and in recent weeks the Sudanese Abdalla."

"*What?* the hit-and-run man?"

"Yes. Officer Migishima had Khan's photograph in connection with the rape allegation. It has now been returned to your section. Obviously, we were not indebted to your files for the photograph of Abdalla, since copies of his passport photograph were supplied to all relevant sections. For your added information, the rape case is now closed for want of an identifiable suspect – and also some doubts about the veracity of the complaint. Most unsatisfactory, but I felt unable to justify further expenditure of manpower on the affair."

Kimura pursed his lips and made a subdued whistling noise, paying no attention to the latter part of what Hara said. "Well, that really *is* interesting, I admit."

"What sort of age? This old grandma." Noguchi was

rubbing a hand over the bumps and craters of his jaws, the friction of his palm on the stubble clearly audible.

Hara nodded vigorously. "I agree that the question is highly relevant. She gave her age as sixty-six. Even if uncorroborated, her evidence is I think worthy of serious consideration. Sixty-six is of course an advanced age, but need not necessarily imply the onset of senility. . ."

Hara's voice trailed away as he and Kimura looked with momentary anxiety at Noguchi, who appeared to be entering the throes of some kind of seizure. The truth dawned upon Kimura first. Ninja Noguchi was laughing. The phenomenon was as brief as it was unprecedented: very soon the noise subsided and he passed the back of his hand across his eyes, then, as if by way of an afterthought, his nose. "Know how old I am, son?" he demanded, but didn't wait for an answer. "Over sixty Ought to have packed up, except the Commander keeps losing my file accidentally on purpose. Know what you mean, though. Touch of senility now and then. Of a Monday morning as a rule."

Hara was mortified. "I assure you, Inspector, I had no –"

Noguchi waved him down as Kimura looked from one to the other of his colleagues, his bright black eyes amused. He could not begin to imagine why Noguchi so obviously liked the sententious, pedantic Hara, but his good humour was catching. Kimura's own long-standing relationship with Noguchi was compounded of elements of real respect and affection and frequent exasperation on both sides, which was usually manifested in heavy, often insulting sarcasm on Noguchi's part and yelps of outrage or protestations of wounded innocence on Kimura's.

"What about this Sudanese Embassy nonsense, Kimura? They shipped the stiff out yet?"

"Yes." Kimura looked down modestly. "I mentioned it to the Old Man when I was having a few drinks with him at his house last night. He thought it a bit fishy too."

Hara coughed gently. "It was perhaps as well that I took the precaution of giving instructions late last Friday for samples

84

of blood and hair to be taken from the body and for a piece of fabric to be cut from the suit he had been wearing." He blinked furiously as Kimura stared at him in stony silence, then continued doggedly. "No doubt, Inspector Kimura, it had occurred to you – "

Kimura interrupted him crossly, thoroughly put out by Hara's foresightedness. "That Abdalla was bogus? Of course it has. And this information from your aged girlfriend – "

"No, no. I have already explained that it was Officer Migishima who – "

Kimura interrupted him in turn by groaning loudly. "It was a joke, Hara. A j-o-k-e. But have it your own way." He began to imitate Hara's own style. "The information vouchsafed to Woman Detective Officer Migishima by a local resident, an elderly lady aged sixty-six who nevertheless appeared to be of active habits and sound mind – "

"Lay off, Kimura." Noguchi sounded irritable again, and Kimura at once reacted to the warning shot.

"All right. Let's start again. Abdalla came here on a scientific scholarship, but did no science before he was killed. Scarcely showed his face on the university campus, in fact. Hardly used the living accommodation provided for him. Now we have evidence – which in fact it ought to be possible to corroborate if we go about it the right way – that he knew Fuhaid well enough to call on him. How many times, Hara? Did the old girl say?"

Hara consulted his notes again. "The word used was 'several', but she was quite decided about the identities of the two men; and indeed I should have made it clear earlier that she picked their photographs out of a considerable number shown to her by Officer Migishima."

Kimura leaned forward and cradled his chin in one hand, his elbow resting on the desk in front of him. It was a newly favoured posture, which he had been struck by while studying with some care the subjects of a "Men of Destiny" series of advertisements for Rolex watches in *Brutus*, the up-market magazine for men. "It struck me early on –" he began, then

85

removed his hand and sat up again on discovering that it was impossible to speak normally as a Man of Destiny. "It occurred to me that Abdalla might not be what he claimed to be. I checked with the Japan Society for the Promotion of Science that in the case of the majority of Third World and all East European nationals receiving scholarships to study or carry out academic research in Japan the right of nomination lies with the sending government. In other words, the JSPS were paying Abdalla – with Japanese government funds of course – but they didn't choose him. The Sudanese Ministry of Education did."

Hara was nodding sagely. "The Sudanese authorities could therefore quite easily have devised a subterfuge whereby they secured a Japanese government scholarship for the real Dr el Abdalla – assuming for the purposes of this discussion that there is a water engineering expert of that name at the University of Khartoum – and substituted someone else, equipped with the necessary passport."

"Why?"

"You mean, why would they want to, Ninja?"

"No sense in it. If they want to send someone here they've only got to make him a diplomat. Half those guys are spooks, everybody knows that. Doesn't even cost a lot when you think how much they make out of flogging duty-free booze and fags."

Hara coughed again. "With respect, Inspector Noguchi, I would suggest that even in Japan there are certain restrictions on the activities of foreign diplomats which do not operate in the case of visiting scholars. There is the additional point that an ostensible member of the Sudanese Embassy would not be able to base himself outside Tokyo. There is, as we know, no Sudanese Consulate in this area."

Kimura tried a different posture, this time making an open steeple with his fingers and peering judiciously over the top. "It is at least an interesting line of speculation. Though we must never forget that Abdalla's death *might* have been accidental."

"And pigs might fly," Noguchi grumbled.

"Anyway, didn't you say something about information through Fuhaid's office, Hara?" Kimura tilted his head courteously towards their new colleague.

"Yes. I am myself at this juncture uncertain of its relevance or value. The receptionist at the company where Fuhaid worked also functions as telephone switchboard operator. She divulged in the course of being questioned about Fuhaid that he rarely received calls which she surmised might be of a personal nature during working hours, except from two women, neither of whom ever volunteered her name. One, she said, was obviously Japanese and possessed a cultivated, assured voice. She sounded like an actress, the girl suggested. The other fairly frequent female caller was a foreigner, speaking good but accented Japanese. Now we are aware that Fuhaid was a divorcee, so there is nothing untoward about his receiving calls from women of his acquaintance."

"Surely she must have listened in now and then? This switchboard girl, I mean. Obviously she'd deny it, but somebody ought to be able to get round her," Kimura said. "I know, why don't I have a word with her myself?"

"Thank you, Inspector, but I have already asked Officer Migishima to gain the young woman's confidence if possible." Hara's manner was prim, with a touch of frost.

"Oh. Oh, well." Kimura shrugged philosophically as Hara droned on.

"It would be safe to assume that these two women are the ones whom the elderly lady witness claimed to have seen visiting Fuhaid at his flat and on occasion going into the building in his company. One, she said, was a Japanese of elegant appearance; the other a foreign woman. Needless to say, she was unable to identify either of them but would, she said, know them at once if she saw them again. The foreign woman was particularly conspicuous, she said, on account of her red hair."

He paused and peered solicitously at Kimura. "Are you feeling quite well, Inspector?" he enquired. "You look pale."

Chapter XII

"Sachiko Chiba? Impossible. Why, she must be in her seventies at least by now. I remember seeing one of her films well before the war when I was a boy, and she was already famous then. An uncle of mine took me: my father wasn't too pleased when he found out. My word, she was beautiful, though." Otani sat back happily in his chair, quite prepared to reminisce, but pulled himself together when he observed the unusually serious expression on Kimura's face.

"It's a different Sachiko Chiba, not the pre-war film star," Kimura said. "This one's a member of the Takarazuka company, so it could well be a stage name, I suppose. I could find out without much difficulty. She's thirty-four."

"Takarazuka? Fancy that." Otani was about to go on and mention his recent impulsive visit to the place, but decided not to. Kimura in glumly businesslike mood had an inhibiting effect. "I thought they were all just young girls in that show. Isn't thirty-four a bit old?"

Kimura sighed. "No, not really. The girls join the company

very young, of course. They never hire established actresses, just kids in their teens. Then they're trained in a kind of school the Takarazuka outfit runs, until those who stay the course are ready to be tried out in the chorus. A lot of them stay at that level, and leave to get married by the time they're in their early twenties, but the promising ones are given featured parts and some of those go on to become stars. Quite a few stay at the top for a good many years, especially the girls who play male roles. Sachiko Chiba's still very popular, but I think she's gradually being phased out as a performer and concentrating on training the younger kids. There's plenty to do – Takarazuka fields four separate companies, you know. Snow, Moon, Flower and Star, they're called. They have a permanent theatre in Tokyo as well as the one here, and go on tour as well."

"Fascinating. How on earth do you know all this, Kimura-kun?"

"Oh, you know how it is, Chief. I've been a bit of a Takarazuka fan for years, and you pick up all sorts of information if you read the articles in the programmes."

Otani looked at him curiously. Something was definitely wrong with Kimura. The usual sparkle was absent, as was the impression of barely suppressed impudence which Otani usually received during their conversations. "I see. Well, how did you get on to this Chiba woman, then?"

They were sitting in their usual chairs by the low coffee table, and Kimura picked up the permanently empty cigarette box on it and fiddled with it irritatingly, opening and closing the lid as he went on. "Ninja and I were having a bit of a discussion with Hara yesterday, and he mentioned that he'd told you about this old woman they got hold of. The one who lives near the Arab's flat. You know, Fuhaid."

"Yes. I had a quick word with Hara before I had to go and see the Governor. It seems that Fuhaid must have had some kind of business with the other fellow, the Sudanese."

"Abdalla."

"Yes. And the Pakistani you talked to. Your report on that

conversation was very interesting, by the way. I've told Hara he must let me have reports in writing on any developments in these cases, too." Otani paused and cleared his throat rather noisily. It had belatedly occurred to him that he seldom if ever made written notes of the progress of his own investigations, and that he had no intention of changing his ways. Furthermore, it was laughable to imagine that Ninja Noguchi might take to the pen.

"Hara told us he'd also reported to you that the old lady said she'd seen two women going to the flat."

"That's right. One Japanese and one foreign. Perhaps you can trace the foreign one, Kimura. Assuming she lives in this area, of course. You'd have her on file, presumably. Though she could easily be registered in Kyoto or Osaka, or even have come down from Tokyo. It's only three hours on the bullet train, after all. She has red hair, apparently."

Kimura opened the cigarette box again, and peered inside. "Yes. I'm working on that, Chief. In fact I went to see this old lady myself. Migishima got the name and address for me from his wife."

"Rather an odd way of going about things. Why didn't you simply ask Hara?"

"He's a bit touchy, you know. I thought it was simpler not to bother him."

Otani exhaled with a show of irritation, but Kimura went on in some haste before he could say anything. "Anyway, I had a word with her to see if she could give me any more information about the foreign woman, and you know how it is with these old dears, they ramble on and she mentioned the Japanese woman, then something about a girl going in and a young man coming out. Hara had mentioned that the switchboard girl at Fuhaid's office said that the Japanese woman who rang him up from time to time talked like an actress, and I had a brainwave."

Otani raised a quizzical eyebrow. "Did you, now? Kimura, would you like a cigarette? You've been playing with that confounded box for the last ten minutes."

Kimura put it down at once. "Sorry. No. No, thanks."

"Well, I'm going to have one myself. I've been trying to do without them except in the open air, but all this is making me a bit confused." Otani went over to his desk and took a Hi-Lite from the packet in his top right-hand drawer. By the time he returned to his easy chair Kimura had his lighter at the ready. Otani sat back in a cloud of smoke. "You had a brainwave," he prompted.

"Yes. It occurred to me that perhaps Fuhaid's Japanese woman friend might *really* be an actress."

"So?"

"So I got the old lady to try to describe her. It was the hair that gave me the idea it might be someone from Takarazuka."

"Why?"

"Because she said that sometimes it was long and sometimes short. You see, the girls who play male roles are specialists. They never appear on stage as women, and so it's convenient for them to have their own hair cut short in male style. It looks quite good with most casual women's clothes too, so it's no problem for them in private life. For the odd formal occasion they can always wear a wig. Well, to cut a long story short, I went back to my place and picked up a souvenir Takarazuka programme I happen to have, and took it to show to the old dear. There are individual photos of all the leading performers, and one or two group pictures of the entire company. It was a long shot, but she picked out Sachiko Chiba at once."

"From a small photo of her in stage make-up and costume? Are you sure she wasn't just trying too hard to be helpful? It all sounds too fanciful for words, Kimura. In any case, even supposing Fuhaid did by some extraordinary chance know this Chiba woman, how does that help us to decide whether or not he committed suicide?"

"It gives us a lead, Chief. We know he was at the hotel in Arima with a woman, and that she apparently vanished off the face of the earth between the time they arrived back in the late afternoon and his body was discovered a few hours later.

Well, suppose it was Sachiko Chiba?"

"And suppose it wasn't?"

"Well, we can't answer either question at the moment. But if it *wasn't*, we ought to be able to eliminate her from the enquiry, because she could presumably prove that she was nowhere near Arima at the material times."

"You're forgetting something, Kimura. Arima isn't very far away from Takarazuka at all. Twenty minutes or so by bus; quite a bit less by car, I should imagine. It might be surprisingly difficult for this lady to produce an alibi, or any of her colleagues for that matter. I really don't think we can rush off and start interrogating Miss Chiba on the strength of the unsupported allegation of some old granny who's had a couple of pages of photographs pushed under her nose. It just won't do, Kimura. What I suggest is that you should forget about her and concentrate on the red-head. Foreigners are your speciality, after all."

Otani looked at his watch and began to haul himself out of his chair. "I must be on my way. I've got to go to the Mayor's press conference. The Kobe Road Safety Week starts tomorrow." He crossed to his old wooden desk and shuffled through the pile of papers on top of the sheet of plate glass which protected its faded green leather surface. "Oh, by the way, Kimura." Kimura paused, his hand on the door-knob. "When did you have your last periodical check-up at the regional police clinic?"

Kimura wrinkled his nose and then rubbed his eyes. "It was in January. The latter half of January. No problems, Chief. Why do you ask?"

"It's nothing. I just thought you were looking a bit seedy, that's all. Are you planning to get away during the Golden Week holidays? Might do you good."

"I'm fine, really. I expect I'll take off somewhere for two or three days. We haven't worked out the leave rota yet."

"No, you're right, we haven't. We must sort it out at the next heads of section meeting. Hang on a second, I'll come downstairs with you."

92

Otani was in uniform that day, and he went over to take his gold-braided cap from its hook at the top of the ancient umbrella stand in the corner near the door, then went out into the corridor, leaving Kimura to close the door after them. They set off along the strip of coconut matting which ran down the centre of the long corridor, on one wall of which were displayed framed photographs of Otani's predecessors as Commander of the Hyogo Prefectural Police Force. He glanced at the picture of one particularly fierce-looking, moustachioed personage. "Ha! I can just see *him* going to a press conference about road safety," he muttered.

Then he put a hand briefly on Kimura's shoulder in what was for him a most uncharacteristic gesture. "It's an interesting theory of yours, I must admit. And the news that Fuhaid and Abdalla had dealings with each other certainly means we can't put the files away yet. Not to mention all this peculiar business about the Sudanese fellow's *bona fides*. I'm hoping that Ninja will come up with something before too long. He's on the track of that taxi-driver."

Chapter XIII

"You know, you're really pretty skinny, Jiro. What you need is a good bowl of chicken noodle soup." Shulamit ran a finger purposefully down Kimura's chest, but he seized her hand and arrested its onward progress.

"I'm sorry," he said. "Nothing like that has happened to me for years."

"Like what? Oh, that! For God's sake, that's nothing to worry about. Gee, I haven't known too many guys who could get it up and keep it up the way you usually do. Want me to try another way?" She smiled at him open-mouthed in the way that he had always previously found extremely exciting, but all at once her red lips looked predatory and he looked away in embarrassment tinged with revulsion.

"Let's wait a while," he said. They were in his own flat, whose neatness and cleanliness always surprised and impressed the women he took there. Kimura seldom stayed in one place very long, being too easily seduced by novelty of any kind, and had occupied his present *manshon* flat for less

94

than a year. There was no doubt that building standards and the quality of the appointments in new apartment blocks were rising all the time, though, and Kimura's restlessness made good financial sense. He had made a tidy profit when disposing of each of the previous flats he had owned on his steady progression up-market, and was currently living on not much more than his salary in a style few of his colleagues could aspire to, even if it was on a comparatively small scale.

"Okay." Shulamit seemed quite equable as she lay back on the bed, idly stroking her own thigh. "I wasn't planning on going no place."

"Now what sort of grammar is that for a Ph.D.?" It was an odd point for Kimura to seize upon, and she turned on her side and scrutinised his face.

"Oh, my," she said. "I beg your pardon, I'm sure, Professor. Only you see, I'm not a Ph.D. yet. I promise I'll talk real pretty when I am." She kissed him, but there was no response, and they both remained silent for a long moment.

"Shulamit."

"Mm?"

"You remember when we went to Takarazuka last Sunday? When you introduced me to Sachiko Chiba?"

"Sure I remember. I hope you aren't going to make a habit of tagging along. It's tough trying to concentrate on my work with you around. Sorry I had to send you away later, but we had serious things to talk about. I structure my interviews very carefully."

She rolled over again, this time half on top of Kimura and scowled at him in mock menace. "Listen, buster. I'm a very jealous lady, and I saw the way you were looking at her. If you're thinking of trying to get into Sachiko's pants, you can think again."

Kimura smiled, looking up into the extraordinary greenish grey of the glowing eyes a few inches above him, and reached up to fish a strand of the fiery red hair from his mouth. "It's nothing like that," he said with some difficulty before heaving her off him and sitting up in bed. "No, I'm just

95

curious. She's your main contact for your research at Takarazuka, I know. You told me. How did you come to meet her in the first place?"

"Oh, it was way back. You know how it is here. Everything has to be done through go-betweens. I thought I could just march into the Takarazuka public relations department, tell them what I wanted and get the sort of help anyone would offer right away in the States. But oh dear no. When I discussed it with my supervising professor at Kobe University he looked stunned, sucked his teeth and then went away for about a week. Then he dredged up a former senior high classmate of his who's a big-shot businessman in Osaka, and this friend introduced me to the president of the Hankyu Railway Company – "

"Who is also the president of Takarazuka Family Land. I get it. No need to go on."

"Pre-cise-lee. I tell you, Jiro, a girl could write a whole Ph.D. dissertation just on the mysteries of getting introduced to Japanese."

"It's been done. There's a Japanese woman professor called Reiko Naotsuka who specialises in that kind of research. You ought to get hold of her books."

Shulamit put her tongue out at him. Since she was still lying on her back in bed and he was sitting up it looked curiously obscene viewed from that angle, and Kimura felt the first flickerings of renewed desire. Perhaps it was all some extraordinary mistake, and the suspicions which made his stomach lurch when he thought about them were quite unfounded. "So. A word from the president and suddenly all doors were open to you at Takarazuka. Right?"

"Right. It was all fixed up for me to visit the training school, and it was Sachiko who either volunteered or was assigned to answer my questions. She speaks pretty good English, and now that she doesn't appear on stage very often she has time. That was months ago, of course."

"You're obviously very close friends now."

"Sure. She's a great girl."

Shulamit's hand was straying up Kimura's leg now, but was abruptly withdrawn as soon as he spoke again. "I'm sorry. I have to ask this. Did you happen to see her in Takarazuka last Friday?"

The American girl swung out of bed without a word, picked up her knickers from the floor and put them on, then reached for the bra hanging over the back of the chair. "Okay, cop," she snapped. "If this is an interrogation, we'll do it with our clothes on."

"Shulamit, listen – "

"Get dressed."

Kimura did as he was told in a tense silence, and was buttoning his shirt as he followed her into the living-room. "Would you like some coffee?" he then asked quietly.

"No. I'd prefer an explanation." She flung herself into the only armchair. "Then I'm going back to my place."

"I didn't mean to make you angry, Shulamit," he said. "In fact I don't understand why you reacted so strongly."

She glared at him, her huge eyes wide. "What in hell did you expect? You invite me back here to screw. Then you can't get it up, and even I can't get it up for you. Okay, something on your mind. Could happen to anybody. Then you start questioning me as though I'm some sort of goddam suspect and wonder why I get mad? All right, mister policeman, just what is all this about? Why are you so curious about Sachiko?"

"I can't tell you that. Not yet, anyway. But her name has come up in connection with a case I'm involved with. I could ask to see her and question her myself, and I may have to. On the other hand you may be able to clear one or two things up which would mean I needn't trouble her. And you were right. Something *is* on my mind. You are. So I have to ask you some questions, Shulamit. If you'll cooperate with me and the answers are what I very much hope they will be, I'll offer you my sincere apologies and ask your forgiveness. But there are some things I have to know. Now. What did you do last Friday?"

Shulamit stared at him coldly for a moment as though he were an importunate stranger, and then began to answer, almost chanting the words. "I got out of bed, went to the bathroom, washed my hair, dressed and made some coffee and toast, then worked in my apartment all morning. Around one I walked down to Sannomiya and ate lunch. Colonel Sanders' Kentucky Fried Chicken, if you want to know what. Used my moneycard to get some money from the bank." She rummaged furiously in her handbag and found her purse, from which she produced a slip of paper which she tried to toss in Kimura's direction: it fluttered to the floor at her feet.

"You want proof? Proof. Dated last Friday. Time, one thirty-eight. Thirty-five thousand yen." Kimura bent to pick up the Dai-ichi Bank notification slip and studied it as Shulamit continued. "Then I went to the university and worked in my study carrel at the library for a couple of hours before going back to the apartment. Instant noodles for early supper before nightfall – it was the beginning of the Sabbath, if you can even begin to understand what that means. Only the God of Israel for a witness. Bed. Alone. Satisfied?"

"You had no contact with Sachiko Chiba that day?"

"No."

"Do you happen to know her teaching schedule for Fridays – or whether last Friday happened to be one of her performance days?"

"No and no. Next question."

Kimura shook his head wearily. "I have no other questions."

Shulamit glared at him, breathing hard. "Well, let me ask one, then. The only sense I can make out of all this stuff about last Friday is that you're trying to prove some theory you've dreamed up about the deaths of those two Moslems. Nothing else special happened that day so far as I know. Am I right?"

"We're investigating two deaths, yes. I told you that last Saturday night. Nobody has so far dreamed up a theory, as you put it."

"Then how on earth did you start imagining that Sachiko or

I might know anything about it? For heaven's sake, I know I sound off about Moslems all the time, but I don't go around killing them, Jiro." Her lip trembled. "You're beginning to scare me."

Kimura moved about the room indecisively. "I don't want to do that. Look, Shulamit, I do have another question after all. I know a little about a lot of the foreigners who live in this area, but there's a great deal I don't know. It's a straight question, and I'm sorry if it upsets you. Were you personally acquainted with either of the two men who died? The one killed by a taxi which didn't stop after it hit him was a Sudanese called Ahmed el Abdalla. The man who died in a hotel at Arima Onsen was an Arab from the Gulf. His name was Hossein Fuhaid."

"Why in the world should I know either of them?"

Shulamit's anger seemed to have given way to a bewildered uneasiness, and Kimura softened his manner, almost pleading with her. "The Sudanese was an academic, attached to Kobe University. You might have encountered him there, or perhaps at a KISS meeting. Hossein Fuhaid was a businessman, and I agree that it would be unlikely for you to have met him casually. Please, Shulamit, if you knew either of them, however slightly, it would help me a lot to know. Or if Sachiko Chiba ever by any chance mentioned having met Fuhaid."

Shulamit passed a hand wearily over her eyes and yawned. "The answer is no to both questions. I never heard of either of them and I'm as sure as hell that Sachiko hasn't."

Kimura was in no doubt that she was dissembling. He never had any difficulty in reading that much in foreigners' faces when they were seeking to mislead him: the problem was that he found it impossible to intuit the truth from their expressions. With Japanese it would be much easier, for though they could lie with marvellous conviction, they also had a strong propensity to confess when put under even moderate psychological pressure.

Even as he stood there looking down at her Kimura was

aware in himself of a powerful urge to tell Shulamit all he knew or thought he knew, and it was only with a conscious effort that he resisted it. For if Fuhaid's two woman acquaintances were in truth Shulamit Steiner and Sachiko Chiba, it was important that they should remain for at least a time in ignorance of the fact that at least one witness had been found who claimed to be able to identify them.

Others must be sought among Fuhaid's neighbours, and the women's photographs would have to be shown to staff at the hotel in Arima where he had died, for however intimately they might have known Fuhaid it was a long step from there to the suggestion that either of them was the mystery woman at the hotel who presumably knew the circumstances of his death. Kimura clung for reassurance to that thought.

Moreover, the diminishing possibility remained that the old lady had been mistaken. Kimura was uncomfortably aware that he had probably drawn her particular attention to the photograph of Sachiko Chiba in the Takarazuka programme even while trying to be dispassionate, and her identification of Shulamit from the small black-and-white passport-style photograph he had shown her had been at best hesitant. It was as well he had said nothing to Otani about that second identification, which really needed to be much more firmly established. A red-headed foreign woman was an uncommon sight, but there were after all thousands of Westerners living in Japan, and there were very probably a number of others with Shulamit's colouring. Fuhaid's visitors could easily have come from Tokyo, as Otani had himself suggested. Would that they had!

Kimura sighed. He seemed to be confronted by blank walls on every side. Perhaps he should have another attempt to persuade the Pakistani Abdul Ghafoor Khan to be more forthcoming: he obviously knew more about the background to the affair than he had thus far divulged.

"I'm still here." Kimura jerked back into attentiveness and refocused on Shulamit: she looked tired and drained, her complexion muddy. "I have to admit I did call a few of my

100

friends about those deaths, Jiro," she said. "Just to find out what rumours might be going around. None of them had ever heard of Fuhaid, but like you said, he was a businessman. Another world, as far as students are concerned." She rubbed her hands together slowly and then clutched at her thin shoulders as though she felt cold.

"As for the Sudanese, el Abdalla. Yes, I did see him one time. He came to a KISS meeting. The one when the Arab bloc tried to vote the Jewish members out. He was introduced at the beginning, but he didn't say a word during the argument: just sat there looking kind of bored. I certainly wasn't about to go up to him afterwards and give him the big hello. I'm sorry he got killed, though. And I'm sorry I got so mad at you, Jiro. I guess you were just doing your job. Damn you, though, why did you have to do it in *bed*?"

Chapter XIV

The head of the Osaka liaison office of the Ministry of Foreign Affairs stretched luxuriously as he and Otani emerged into the sunshine from the New Port Hotel where they had attended the weekly meeting of the Rotary Club of Kobe South, of which Otani was proud to be a member, even though he had over the years been several times taken to task concerning his less than exemplary attendance record.

"It was good of you to spare the time to be my guest today," Otani said politely.

"No problem," his companion said in his unvarnished way. "The food isn't much worse than we get in the big city." Ambassador Atsugi was a big, expansive man and grinned down at Otani who, although a man of normal enough height for a Japanese of his generation, looked quite diminutive at the side of the diplomat.

Both men were wearing dark suits with their Rotary badges winking at the lapel, but instead of the conventional white shirt Atsugi was wearing one made of blue linen and with a button-down collar which made him look to Otani like one of the second- or third-generation Americans of Japanese descent who not infrequently turned up at the Kobe South Club while on package holidays in Japan. On the other hand, he reflected as they turned away from the harbour and headed for Sannomiya Station, Americans even with racial connections with Japan didn't seem to bring decent suits with them; they wore the sort of clothes he associated with Japanese golfers.

"You wouldn't believe the amount of chicken à la king I ate at Rotary meetings when I was Consul General in Los Angeles." Atsugi strolled along in what looked like a leisurely way, but Otani was hard put to keep up with him. "It quite took me back, especially talking with those two American Rotarians. Who'd have thought there'd be a Rotary Club in Snowball, Arkansas?" Atsugi's last remark was complete gibberish to Otani, who was startled when his distinguished friend burst briefly into song in a fruity baritone and greatly relieved when he stopped again.

Otani liked the diplomat in spite of his breezy, un-Japanese ways, and although hesitating to trouble him had been delighted by his ready response to the suggestion that they might have lunch together. "It was a pleasant coincidence that you had to come to Kobe today anyway. A conference, I think you said, on Port Island?"

They had not really had a chance to talk during the one-hour lunch meeting, what with the business of introductions and the singing of the National Anthem followed by "Happy Birthday" in English to several Rotarians, one of whom, an elderly company president, nearly broke down with emotion and made a special donation of fifty thousand yen towards the mobile X-ray unit the Club was planning to present to the municipal authorities.

There had followed the routine announcements, then the hastily served lunch during which Atsugi chatted affably in English to the two Arkansan Rotarians across the table, and finally the weekly talk. This was by a representative of an

103

agricultural cooperative in nearby Wakayama Prefecture who explained with passion why it would be disastrous to liberalise the import of American beef into Japan, thus causing much embarrassment to those in the neighbourhood of the two representatives of the Rotary Club of Snowball, Arkansas, who had only minutes earlier presented a miniature replica of their club pennant to the President and received Kobe South Club pennants in return.

"That's right. At the new Conference Centre right by the Portopia Hotel." Atsugi extended a hairy wrist from his expensively tailored sleeve and consulted his watch. "My, my. You people really keep a tight schedule, don't you? It's only one thirty-five now. I'm not due at the conference until just before three. Feel like riding the Portliner train out there with me? It's a nice afternoon. Or we could take a cab."

Otani had been hoping for this. "Excellent. Let's take the Portliner by all means. I enjoy the view." It was less than five minutes' walk straight up the broad boulevard from the hotel to the terminus, and they were already half-way there. "I'm glad of an opportunity to have an informal word with you," Otani began, considering it quite time to come to the point.

"Sure, sure. I assumed you had something on your mind. And I'll make a guess it's connected with these two dead Arabs of yours."

Otani smiled. "A guess?"

"An informed guess, shall we say. After all, my people did have to notify the Sudanese and United Arab Emirates Embassies via Tokyo. They have no consular representatives down here in the Kansai, as you know."

"Of course. Well, there are some odd aspects to these cases which may or may not amount to anything. We're working on the theory that the Sudanese was killed deliberately. We've got nowhere in the matter of motive, because even making allowances for the fact that he'd only been here a few weeks, he was something of a mystery man."

"Uh huh. And his embassy shipped his body out in something of a hurry, I heard."

"Yes. The thought has occurred to us that he might not have been what he claimed to be. He was here on a research scholarship but hadn't done any scientific work whatsoever up to the day he was killed. And although he had been allotted a small apartment in the foreign researchers' guesthouse he hardly ever seemed to use it. There was next to nothing in the way of personal belongings there when my people looked it over, and a man from the Sudanese Embassy took even those away shortly afterwards. I can only assume he stayed somewhere else most of the time, and I'm wondering if it was in Tokyo."

Atsugi grunted but made no reply as they negotiated the permanently busy Sannomiya crossing, entered the Portliner terminus, bought their tickets from the machine and settled in the comfortable, driverless train which, they were advised by loudspeaker announcement, was due to depart in three minutes. Both men studied their fellow passengers, a mixed bag of young housewives with small children, one or two old people and a young foreign couple, dressed as though for mountaineering in huge boots and with ungainly back-packs which they kept on throughout the ride.

"Otani-san. I wonder what they think they're going to find at the other end?" Atsugi whispered hoarsely. "Alpine meadows and quaint country ways?"

Otani smiled, but tightly. The investigations which he had perhaps unnecessarily taken it upon himself to supervise seemed to be leading all of them into some strange and tortuous byways, most of which led to the closed and alien world symbolised by the squat, incongruous Kobe Mosque. "I expect they're carrying all their belongings with them," he said. "A lot of young foreigners seem to do that when they come here. I suppose it's reasonable enough when you come to think about it." He was thinking ruefully about the crisis in the Otani household the previous year caused by the arrival of their first foreign house guest, the English girl Rosie Winchmore, when the doors hissed shut and the train glided out of the terminus on its rubber-tyred wheels past the Trade

Centre building to begin its computer-controlled circular journey round Port Island.

Like all Japanese Otani was inured to the almost incessant recorded announcements made on all forms of public transport which fussily informed passengers what the name of the next stop was, told them which side the doors would open and reminded them to take their belongings with them when getting off. On first riding the Portliner, though, he had been taken aback to realise that the recorded messages were in English as well as Japanese, the girl's voice on the tape being without doubt that of a genuine American.

"I had a look at the outside of the mosque earlier today," he said abruptly. "It's a very peculiar sort of place. The side street it stands in is quite narrow. A more or less square building, about fifteen metres each way I suppose, and about twelve metres high not counting a sort of dome on top. I'm told by Inspector Hara that there's very little to see inside. Have you met him yet, by the way?"

"Your new boy from Nagasaki? No. But I've heard about him. The word is he did a great job organising the local security for the Pope's visit there a few years back. Made himself quite an expert on Catholic doctrine, I'm told. Just in case he got to meet the man himself."

"That sounds like him. He's an expert on Islam now. Noguchi likes him."

"He does? Wonders will never cease. Let me ask you something. Do you think the other fellow was murdered too?"

Otani's quiet voice had been virtually inaudible to anyone but Atsugi over the rumble of the train as it slid smoothly out beside the port area, the sea blue in the bright April sunshine; but Atsugi's normal speaking voice carried remarkably and an old lady sitting opposite the two men gaped at him nervously and moved to a vacant seat further along. "Perhaps we'd better wait till we get off," Otani suggested. "Ours is the next stop anyway. It really is a beautiful day. Should be quite hot by Golden Week."

106

Atsugi nodded and reached down to scratch his calf above his bright red socks. "You know, I really envy you, working in Kobe. I can't wait to get out of Osaka."

"They used to call it the Venice of the Orient once," Otani said. "Before they built the motorways over all the canals – "

" – which stink to high heaven in the summer. I know."

Very few passengers seemed to be bound for the hotel and conference centre, and when Otani and Atsugi emerged from the small station at ground level they were the only pedestrians in the area. The great glass cliff of the Portopia Hotel loomed up on their left as Otani led the way to the fountains in the South Park at the very extremity of the artificial island, from where there is an uninterrupted view of the whole magnificent sweep of the harbour and of the Inland Sea beyond.

"I came here during the Portopia Exposition a few times," Atsugi said after appreciatively sucking in several huge lungfuls of the clean sea air. "It's a whole lot better without any people."

Otani stirred the gravel with the toe of one highly polished shoe, grateful for the sense of solitude and space. "Yes. There are very few people about here in the middle of the week. You were asking about the second death. The Arab in the hotel at Arima. I'm doing my best to keep an open mind about it, at least until we manage to track down a woman who was presumably the last person to see him alive. In any case, I quite see that one shouldn't automatically infer a connection between the two deaths. All the same it's difficult to avoid doing so in the circumstances."

Atsugi raised a bushy eyebrow. "Supposing they'd died several days or weeks apart? Would it even have *occurred* to you to pay particular attention to the fact that they both happened to be Moslems? I rather fancy not."

"I don't know. It might. Especially as we have evidence that the two men knew each other. I'm not sure yet how well."

Atsugi shrugged and they walked a few yards along the sea wall. "If I know you at all, you'll come up with something sooner or later, Otani-san. Certainly I can think of plenty of motives for Moslems to murder each other, though it would have been pretty clever on the part of your two to have achieved it."

"Political *and* religious motives, I suppose you mean."

"Right. I don't envy you the job of teasing them out, though."

Otani gazed out towards a container ship low in the water, moving almost imperceptibly towards the new terminal. "May I ask your help on the political side?"

"Why not? Go ahead."

"I wonder if you'd be good enough to have your people in Tokyo look into the business of the Sudanese? Maybe they could throw some light on it, or at the very least tie up one troublesome loose end by confirming that the man was a genuine scientist. Would it be possible to get our ambassador in the Sudan to make a discreet enquiry about him at the university there? I don't like to suggest to the experts what to do, but. . ."

"All the same you know what you'd like done, right? I'll see what I can arrange. Anything for a brother Rotarian. What else?"

"Nothing else. Thank you. I shall be very grateful for any help you can give me. In confidence, needless to say. If and when we get to the stage of making an arrest I'd ask you to look at the report to the District Prosecutor in draft and clear it."

The diplomat looked at Otani's earnest expression and grinned suddenly. "Gee, thanks," he said in English, then looked at his watch again before reverting to Japanese. "Look, I'd better get over to the conference centre. There are one or two people I have to get a word with before the session actually starts. And I'll call a friend of mine at the Ministry in Tokyo about your little problem. Will you walk across with me?"

Otani gave his head a little shake as though to clear it, then looked up at the big man. "If you don't mind, I think I'll stroll

108

about here for a while longer. Ambassador, you will let me know if you find out anything, won't you?"

Atsugi nodded, a half smile on his fleshy face, and then clapped Otani on the shoulder in a friendly way, a gesture Otani was becoming quite used to from him. "I'll do that," he promised. "Don't fall in the sea now." Then he had turned on his heel and was striding away to the conference centre adjoining the hotel.

By the time Otani's aimless wanderings had brought him to the entrance to the Portopia Funfair, closed and deserted on this mid-week off-season day, the two young foreigners who had been on the train had completed their circuit of the pleasantly unfussy park area and were standing with their arms awkwardly round each other's backsides in spite of the cumbersome back-packs, contemplating the impressionistic scale model of the Kobe area worked in granite as part of a rock-garden not far from the next station on the Portliner loop line.

There was nobody else about, and the couple gazed with some interest at the tidily dressed, middle-aged Japanese who was so obviously lost in thought – until he suddenly stopped short, blinked, looked around and then made hurriedly for the station entrance. There were public telephones there, and Otani had an important call to make.

Chapter XV

Inspector Ninja Noguchi descended in stately fashion from the bus and sniffed the air. The rain of the previous day had washed the air, and only a few puffballs of cloud drifted in a sky whose blue was already noticeably richer than the clear eggshell of winter. He was glad of the returned warmth and higher humidity: the dry chill of winter nights seemed to bring on the bronchitis that troubled him a little more every year. He turned left at the cross-roads and entered a smaller street too narrow to boast a sidewalk. Instead a broad white line was painted on the left-hand side to indicate the pathway supposedly reserved for pedestrians and cyclists, but which was in fact completely blocked by parked cars.

Even had it been clear there were hazards enough for the unwary, because, as in the street in which Ahmed el Abdalla had died and in virtually every other residential area in Japan, massive concrete electricity-supply poles reared up every hundred yards or so in the pedestrian pathway. Many had small notices flyposted to them, and these fell into two categories.

The political kind had been placed by extremist right-wing political organisations and were cheaply printed in monochrome. They peremptorily demanded the immediate return to Japanese sovereignty of the four islands north of Hokkaido currently under Soviet control, or the passage of an anti-espionage law by the National Diet. More rarely they announced public meetings to be addressed by such unrepentant imperialists as the veteran agitator Bin Akao or to mark the anniversary of the suicide of the novelist Yukio Mishima in 1970.

The other kind were gaudily printed in three colours and advertised live sex shows at a local strip theatre. The current one featured girls from "four foreign countries" – almost certainly a Korean, a Filipina, a Taiwanese and a Thai, but just possibly and at considerably greater expense a lone European or American – and both "black-white" or heterosexual and "white-white" or lesbian sex.

Even though the road was full of men going in the same direction, hardly any of them paid the slightest attention to the posters. This was because most of them were absorbed in the study of the closely printed sheets of papers which were sold here and there by men sitting on upturned crates with piles of them held in place by a stone. Noguchi paused to buy one himself but then stuffed it unread into his jacket pocket. The bicycle racing was due to start in about twenty minutes.

Both the surroundings and the people in this drab part of the Western outskirts of Kobe were a far cry from those to be found a couple of miles east in the fashionable shopping centres of Motomachi and Sannomiya and the prosperous residential suburbs of Nada, Rokko and Nishinomiya. It was as though the part through which Noguchi was walking had grown weak and pale from loss of blood. The flashy posters advertising the sex shows were among the few touches of colour in the street of wooden houses and open-fronted shops, which themselves seemed to display their wares in a listless, half-hearted way.

111

The men on their way to win or lose a few thousand yen at the race track were of all ages, but predominantly in their thirties and forties, and were for the most part poorly dressed in cheap, ill-fitting clothes or, in the case of the younger ones, self-consciously flashy in sharp, *yakuza*-style suits. Noguchi knew better than most that some of these were in fact *chinpira*, the lowest-ranking errand boys of the real gangsters, but that most were probably garage hands or dishwashers who lived quite quietly at home with their parents.

Noguchi himself was dressed in the clothes he usually wore. He therefore fitted in perfectly and nobody gave him a second look as he paid at the turnstile and entered the modest arena. Loudspeakers were squawking and crackling but Noguchi could make little sense of what was being said as he looked around to see if he recognised any acquaintances, then pulled the form sheet from his pocket and glanced through it. For the first race he decided to put a thousand yen on a cyclist whose name he happened to have heard mentioned the previous evening in a Korean snack bar specialising in grilled liver and kidneys. To his pleased surprise he won four thousand yen – enough to buy him his simple lunch for a week. He was brooding more seriously over his selection for the second race when a dirty finger stabbed at the paper in his hand, pointing out a name.

"Can't go wrong," a hoarse voice insisted.

Noguchi replied without turning his head. "What about that horse you tipped me six months ago? Still running, I shouldn't be surprised."

"Somebody got at him. Bit of bad luck. Have I ever let you down before?" Noguchi emitted a mirthless grunt which nevertheless sounded more or less good-humoured, and only then turned slowly to contemplate the wizened little man at his side.

He might have been anything from forty to sixty, and looked a little like one of the wooden *kokeshi* dolls sold in souvenir shops all over the country, with his round bald head and thin arms now tucked stiffly into his sides. "All right. If I

112

lose, it comes off your grease, right?" Noguchi set off to the window to place his bet, the little man trailing along behind complaining. He took his own advice, though, producing a dirty, crumpled thousand-yen note of his own to match Noguchi's wager; and they had no further conversation until the race was over.

"Your lucky day, Uncle," Noguchi said in high good humour when their man won. His companion beamed gummily and they set off to collect their winnings, after which Noguchi bought them each a tiny bottle of vitamin drink and led the way to a part of the guard rail well away from the finish line where it was crowded. "All right," he said then. "It checked out." He took an envelope from his inside pocket with his left hand and slid it under his right arm. It vanished at once into Uncle's capacious coat.

"Knew it would. Worth more than a lousy fifty thou, that. I could have got more than that off the foreman if I'd leaned on him a bit."

"Oh no you couldn't," Noguchi said benignly. "You'd have got your empty head bashed in, that's what. With a spanner. Who do you fancy for the next race?"

Uncle sniffed in outrage. "Hark at him! Talk about sauce! Done all right today you have, thanks to me. Any more tips'll cost you."

Noguchi gazed at him expressionlessly. "Thought as much. Right, piss off, Uncle. See you around." Then he swung a pretend punch at the little man, who briefly adopted a fighting stance and danced about in a very spry fashion for a few seconds before winking at Noguchi and melting away into the crowd.

Noguchi stayed where he was, looking out over the track and seeing without paying attention to two more races as he pondered his next move. The maintenance foreman of the taxi firm whose garage was only two blocks away from the Kobe Mosque had at first righteously denied that any of the vehicles being serviced the previous Friday had been unaccounted for at any time during the day. The daily work-

113

sheets had shown that there were in any case only three, and although they were all out on the road again it was a simple matter for the Hyogo police traffic department to instruct the firm's manager to have the three drivers called in by radio.

Careful examination of the front offside wings of the three taxis had revealed no trace of blood or hair: the police had not expected it to. However, among the fibres extracted from the rim of the headlight of one of them were two which matched those of the strip of fabric snipped on Inspector Hara's instructions from an inside seam of the dead man's suit. There was also a slight dent in the wing which might or might not have been caused by impact with a human body.

Armed with the report of the regional forensic laboratory, Hara's staff had interviewed the foreman and the two mechanics employed full-time in the servicing bay at the garage and uncovered their modest but quite lucrative sideline in hiring out for a few hours at a time, usually overnight or at weekends, to freelance drivers taxis which were officially out of service. Fixing the meters and turning back the mileage readings to make them tally with their regular drivers' daily work-sheets was a relatively simple business for experts with the right tools and equipment on hand.

On Noguchi's advice and with Hara's very reluctant consent a deal was struck with the foreman and the mechanics. The police would turn a blind eye to their fiddle on two conditions: that they put an end to it forthwith and that they helped to identify the person who had taken out on the previous Friday the taxi which had been used to kill the Sudanese. The first condition was accepted at once in a chorus of eager insincerity, but the second led to honest head-shaking. Identification was another matter altogether.

The hirer had "booked" the cab for two hours over Friday lunchtime by telephone, mentioning the name of the friend who had given him the foreman's name. He had asked for the cab to be parked in an unrestricted residential street not far from the garage, with the keys in the glove compartment, and agreed to return it to the same spot with the fee stowed in the same place. It was the usual arrangement, and one which minimised risk: it was normal routine for one of the mechanics to take a newly serviced vehicle out for a road test, whereas a stranger wandering into the garage would be noticed. The foreman therefore had no idea who had in fact driven the car that day. He knew only that it had been back in place by the appointed time with the money tucked away in the glove compartment with the keys. The mechanic who went to pick it up recalled that the number plates had been filthy and agreed that it seemed possible that they had been deliberately obscured.

Noguchi had been involved in the second round of questioning and had taken it upon himself to have a word with the "friend" whose name the anonymous hirer of the taxi had mentioned to the foreman by way of establishing his credentials, and which the foreman passed on to Noguchi with the utmost reluctance and an expression on his face which suggested that he already felt quite unwell.

Noguchi's reassurances to him at that time had been perfectly genuine, though, for he was acquainted with the "friend" in question and had quite enough on him to be able to request a little information from him in confidence. The man had been out of town for a couple of days, but was due back later that afternoon, and Noguchi planned to be at the *pachinko* pinball parlour he owned to welcome him back and to invite him out for a few drinks.

The day had started well, and it promised to be an interesting evening. Inspector Noguchi was therefore in a cheerful mood as he checked to make sure that his winnings were safely tucked away in his purple woollen belly-band, and then made for the exit gate to go in search of some lunch.

Chapter XVI

"Mr Abdul Ghafoor Khan, sir," Kimura said stiffly as he opened the door to Otani's office. Otani knew that Kimura was much offended by his decision to interview the Pakistani himself, but had been firm in pointing out that although he did not doubt Kimura's claim that the man habitually spoke English, as a trader long resident in Japan Khan must be equally at home in Japanese. Had he not indeed volunteered to use that language when he first met Kimura?

"Good afternoon. Otani is my name. I am pleased to meet you," he said politely to the stranger, then turned at once to Kimura. "Please stay, Inspector. I should be grateful if you would." He then ushered the Pakistani to the chair always occupied by Noguchi during their conferences, leaving Kimura to take his own habitual place. "It was very good of you to spare the time to come to see us here."

"Not at all. I am of course most anxious to cooperate in your enquiries in every way."

However much he prepared himself for the experience, it

116

always came as a surprise to Otani when a foreigner demonstrated the ability to speak Japanese. Khan's was correct, and with only a trace of an accent. Furthermore, Kimura's briefing had led Otani to expect a demonstrative sort of person dressed in loud clothes, whereas on this occasion Khan was wearing an impeccably sober dark grey suit with a white shirt and a dark blue tie with unobtrusive red dots scarcely bigger than pinheads. His manner was gracefully courteous, and Otani looked at him with approval, much more at ease with him than he was ever able to be with Westerners who never seemed to know where to put their feet or hands and who usually conveyed to Otani a sense of barely suppressed violence.

"I'm sure you do. My colleagues and I are making very satisfactory progress in our investigations, and expect to be in a position to make an arrest very soon." Kimura almost bit his tongue in preventing himself from interrupting, while Abdul Ghafoor Khan's eyes widened and he leant forward in his chair with a jerk, opening his mouth to speak.

Otani went blandly and insistently on. "I refer of course to the hit-and-run killing of Dr Ahmed el Abdalla. The taxi has been identified: it belongs not to an owner-driver but to a company, and had been stolen from their garage where it had lately been serviced. It has now been recovered. I am sure you and your fellow-members of the Islamic community here will be relieved to know that the person responsible for the death of Dr Abdalla will without doubt soon be identified and be made to face the consequences of his action."

Abdul Ghafoor Khan licked his lips rapidly with a flickering lizard tongue, and nodded several times. "Indeed, yes, Superintendent. The efficiency of your men is much to be commended. But, if I may say so, I – "

"You had not expected to talk about the late Dr el Abdalla? No, of course not. I must apologise for mentioning his tragic death first. The breakthrough of which I have just been speaking has not unnaturally placed the matter in the forefront of my mind. In fact I believe you telephoned my

117

colleague Inspector Kimura to say that you had some information to pass on relating to the death later the same day of Mr Hossein Fuhaid?"

"Yes, sir. The fact is. . .it seems absurd to put it like this, but. . .I have received a letter. From Mr Fuhaid."

There was a long silence before Otani spoke. "I should like to be quite clear that I have understood you, Mr Khan. You have received a letter from Hossein Fuhaid? Recently?"

"Yes, sir, I have. This morning. But according to the postmark, it was mailed last Friday."

"A whole week ago?" The tension was diminished, but Otani's tone remained sceptical. Such a delay between posting and delivery was not unheard of, but was sufficiently unlikely for him at once to conclude that the Pakistani had held on to the letter for a reason.

"How very strange. May I see it, please?"

"Of course. Though the text is in Arabic."

Khan's long thin face was as expressionless as Otani's own as he reached into the inside pocket of his jacket and took out an ordinary envelope in one of the standard sizes approved by the postal authorities. One end of it had been neatly sliced off with scissors. Otani first scrutinised the envelope, which bore an ordinary rate sixty-yen stamp and was indeed clearly postmarked "Arima, 20 IV 59". He turned it over, reflecting as he did so that it was hard to believe that it really was the fifty-ninth year of the old Emperor's reign.

There was no return address on the back: this omission was in breach of postal regulations and might, Otani supposed, be one cause of delay in handling. Another might be the fact that it was addressed in Roman script; in theory perfectly acceptable to the Japanese post office but in practice exceedingly difficult for the average sorting office employee to cope with unless typewritten. This envelope was defaced by an ugly, handwritten scrawl which Otani for one was completely unable to decipher, though he could see that the address lacked a postal code number.

Otani frowned as he extracted and unfolded the single

sheet of paper which the envelope contained, then handed the empty envelope to Kimura. A week's delay in delivery of such a missive sent from a hot-spring resort off the international tourist track no longer seemed remarkable to him. He looked with interest at the graceful, swooping curves of the writing on the paper. They meant nothing to him, but were much more pleasing to the eye than the Roman script of the envelope. "Well, Mr Khan. Will you be good enough to tell me what the letter says?"

Abdul Ghafoor Khan coughed delicately behind one slim, bony hand. "It is a farewell letter. In effect, a suicide note. Please understand, sir, that my own knowledge of written Arabic is slight, and largely derived from religious texts. Of the spoken language it is virtually nil."

"May I see the letter for a moment, sir?" It was Kimura, speaking in the official style he used in addressing Otani only in the presence of an outsider or when he had reason to be apologetic about something. Otani handed it over. Kimura looked at it, and then again at the envelope before handing them both back to Otani who placed them on the coffee table between them and looked at the Pakistani thoughtfully before snapping his fingers and tut-tutting.

"I'm so sorry, Mr Khan. It is very remiss of me not to have offered you some green tea. Inspector, I wonder if you would be so kind. . . ?"

Grimly, Kimura rose and went to the anteroom to instruct Otani's clerk to bring refreshments. He could not fathom the logic of Otani's approach to Khan, and deplored his having mentioned the matter of Noguchi's breakthrough at all, let alone at the outset of the conversation. From his quick look at the letter and the envelope in which it had been delivered Kimura was reasonably persuaded that the same fine black felt-tipped pen had been used to write both, though it would take a particularly skilled handwriting expert to decide with confidence whether the scrawled address and the Arabic of the enclosed letter had been penned by the same hand. There was certainly no doubt about the authenticity of the postmark. Kimura's mind was racing round the problem of how to set about obtaining a certified translation of the letter as he went back into Otani's office and returned to his chair.

"Ah, there you are, Inspector. I was just asking Mr Khan whether it surprised him to receive a letter from his friend written in Arabic." Abdul Ghafoor Khan still looked to Kimura somehow diminished in his sober suit, and now that he was speaking Japanese his remarks lacked the confident zest which had characterised the English he had used at the Oriental Hotel. "He said no, not given the circumstances."

Khan nodded. "When in each other's company we habitually used English. We never had occasion to write to each other. This letter was written by a man at the end of his tether, though. Anyone writing such a note would naturally use his own language. Hossein would have known that I would be able to understand what he wrote."

The tea arrived, and Otani gestured hospitably to the other two men as he picked up his own cup and sniffed appreciatively at the familiar fragrance. Hanae bought the tea for him, from a specialist shop in Osaka. It was of superior quality, from Uji near Kyoto, and he didn't begrudge the cost even though he knew that its quality was wasted on most of his guests, especially Noguchi.

"The letter is without question your property," he said after a preliminary sip. "And it will be returned to you in due course. We should however be grateful if you would leave it and the envelope with us for the time being, please. You will appreciate that we must have it translated into Japanese by an independent interpreter. I will gladly have photocopies made for you to take with you if you wish." Khan nodded rather distractedly, his eyes closed. "For the moment, though, would you be so kind as to let us have a very rough literal translation? The text appears to be quite brief."

The Pakistani opened his eyes again and took up the sheet of paper with a little sigh. "Yes, yes," he muttered. "I'll leave it with you of course." He squinted slightly at the letter, held it out almost at arm's length and then sighed again. "I don't have my glasses with me, but I'll try to manage. He begins in the Islamic style by greeting me and assuring me of his affection. Conventional phrases, you understand. Then goes on to say that he has been under intolerable strain, undergoing many tribulations and moreover great anxiety about his health. He thanks me for my friendship during the time. . ." His voice cracked slightly and he paused before going on. ". . . Friendship during the period he lived in Kobe, and asks me to convey his respectful farewells to the Imam and to the congregation at the Kobe Mosque. We shall meet again, he says, in Paradise." He looked up, his great brown eyes swimming. "An indisputable suicide note," he said.

"It certainly sounds like it," Otani said. Then he continued in what Kimura was distinctly shocked to note was an almost cosy manner. "Now, Mr Khan, I'd like your purely personal opinion. Can you think of any genuine reason – convincing to you, I mean – why Hossein Fuhaid might have killed himself? Oh, and another question, why do you think somebody had Abdalla killed?" Khan gulped at his tea, which was still quite hot, and spluttered as it scalded his throat. He produced a paper handkerchief from his trouser pocket and dabbed at his eyes.

"I have done my best to translate my friend's letter for you, Superintendent," he said, after recovering his poise. "I am quite confident that your official translator, whoever he may be, will not produce any significantly different version. Ill-health, anxiety, and so on. He gives no other reason, and I see no occasion to look for one." He pursed his thin lips before continuing. "As to Abdalla, I said at the beginning that I am anxious to cooperate, but I do not understand why you insist on repeatedly bringing up his name. I scarcely ever met the man. You appear to be insinuating that I know something about his death."

"I am very sorry if I have given you that impression," Otani said contritely. "Nothing could have been further from my intentions. We count on your friendly assistance, I assure you. Let me put my questions in another way. From your broad acquaintance with many members of the Islamic community in Kobe, would you consider that there might be any likelihood of a connection between the death of Ahmed el Abdalla and that of Hossein Fuhaid a few hours later?"

This time Khan appeared to give the question sober and obective consideration. "How could there be?" he said at last. "Abdalla died – "

"Was killed."

"Was killed in a traffic accident in Kobe; while Hossein took his own life in Arima, miles away. We in the mosque congregation have of course discussed the tragedies among ourselves, assuming that they were an unhappy coincidence."

"Ah. I see. I can well imagine that there must have been a great deal of talk about all this unhappy business."

Otani turned to Kimura. "Inspector Kimura. Would you be so kind as to show Mr Khan the objects we were discussing earlier?" Kimura had a simple pocket file with him, in a strident shade of orange. He opened it with a dubious glance at Otani and took out a plastic bag which he opened in turn, tipping the contents out on to the coffee table beside the suicide letter.

"The wallet is now empty," Otani explained helpfully. "Everything which was in it is now on the table with the other things." Khan leaned forward and peered at the unimpressive collection of bits and pieces on the table. Apart from the wallet, a tawdry-looking thing made of plastic simulating leather, there were three keys on a ring whose tag showed that it was a souvenir of the tourist city of Nara, a few notes and coins amounting in all to a comparatively modest sum, a Citizen brand wristwatch of the less expensive kind, an Alien Registration Card and some odds and ends like name-cards, receipts and a few crumpled paper handkerchiefs.

"These things were found in Hossein Fuhaid's clothing," Otani said. "His passport has not been found in his apartment; nor anything in the way of a bank passbook, credit cards or other personal papers. In addition to searching his home, my officers have of course also examined the contents of his desk at the office where he worked. He kept a file of name-cards there as many business people do: all obviously related to his work. Nothing personal of any kind, though. These two name-cards were in his wallet. One of Dr el Abdalla's – and one of yours. Now why do you suppose he carried about just those two?"

Khan shook his head. "I have no idea. Of course I gave him one of my cards when I first met him, and he let me have one of his. It's the custom here. We soon became very good friends – "

"Exactly. Such good friends that when Fuhaid wrote a suicide note it was to you that it was sent. He was I understand a divorced man with no relations in Japan, yet with all respect to you one would have expected such a note to be addressed to someone. . .closer to him, in his home country probably. And that makes it all the odder for him to have been carrying your card. A person might well need to refer to the name-card of a business contact or casual acquaintance, to check his telephone number, for example. In the case of a close friend, though? And why should he have Abdalla's card?"

Kimura couldn't prevent himself from chipping in. "Why not? Abdalla had only just arrived, and would obviously have been passing out cards to everybody he met –"

"Thank you, Inspector, but I'd prefer to have Mr Khan's opinion." Otani's tone was icy and Kimura subsided, his lips compressed.

"Mr Khan, were you perhaps the person who actually introduced Abdalla to Fuhaid?" Khan's tongue flickered round his dry lips again as he looked from one to the other of the two police officers, Otani in uniform and Kimura in a lightweight Italian suit which he had bought two years previously but thought might just be worn for one more season without embarrassment.

"Now that you mention it, I suppose I may have been."

"I see. So Abdalla went along to the mosque for Friday prayers, and you spotted that he was a stranger. You made haste to welcome him and make him feel at home, gave him

123

one of your name-cards and introduced him to Fuhaid and perhaps others? Could it have been like that, Mr Khan?"

Irritated though he was at being upstaged by the Old Man, Kimura had to admire the way he had mastered the foreign names and came out with them so confidently, without even glancing at the notes on the clip-board at the side of his chair.

"Perhaps. I really can't remember."

"What a pity. And we still don't know why your good friend had a copy of your name-card in his wallet, do we?"

"Unless he carried it about with the idea of recommending your tailoring firm to people he met, Mr Khan?" Kimura was again only trying to be helpful, and was hurt by the withering smile Otani aimed at him.

"That may have been it, of course," Otani said thinly. "Well, Mr Khan, we mustn't detain you. The letter you have brought to our attention is of the highest importance, and we are most grateful to you. We might very possibly need to have a further word with you after this – I take it that you have no plans to leave Kobe in the near future?"

"No. No, I have no business trips planned for the next few weeks."

"Good. Now if I may trouble him once more, Inspector Kimura will escort you out."

As he waited for Kimura to return, Otani peered again at the letter from Hossein Fuhaid. He did not know how Kimura planned to get it translated, but thought it might be a good idea to ask the Imam at the mosque to oblige. There were one or two questions he wanted put to the translator, whoever it was.

Chapter XVII

"Don't apologise, Inspector. It's an old building, after all."
Otani settled himself comfortably in the only easy-chair in the
one and only private office at the Takarazuka police station
and looked around him with approval. He liked the old silk-
backed scroll hanging on one wall. It was executed with no
more than a few strokes of the ink-brush but the depiction of a
Zen priest and an appealing frog looking at each other
quizzically was masterly; bursting with vivid life and humour.

On the window-sill was an open fan on a bamboo stand.
The background of the stiff paper was creamy white with the
glossy black lacquer spines of the frame in severe and
disciplined contrast, the design a brilliant slash of pink, an
impressionist cherry blossom. There was a bonsai in a shallow
bowl on top of the filing cabinet; a miniature red pine which
Otani would have given a lot to be able to add to his own small
collection. In short, although small and crowded, it was a
room a man could think in, and told him far more about
Yasuo Sugawa than the personnel record file which he had

125

looked through before leaving Kobe to refresh his memory about the Divisional Inspector.

It was all very well for Hanae to boast gently, as she sometimes did, about the fact that he was in command of the third largest police force in Japan in terms of manpower; but what she sometimes failed to realise was that Hyogo Prefecture was so huge in area, covering not only Kobe City and the many dormitory suburbs around, but other major towns like Himeji and Akashi on the coastline of the Inland Sea, Wakayama and Toyooka in the mountains to the north and Kasumi and Hamasaki up in the national park area of the Japan Sea coast. Not to mention substantial places like Takarazuka which attracted thousands of visitors nearer home. Otani summoned his dozens of divisional inspectors to Kobe for occasional conferences, even though that was an expensive business which from time to time led to arguments with the finance committee of the Hyogo Public Safety Commission, but during the years of his command had not managed to visit all of them on their home ground.

"You've been here almost two years now, Inspector."

After a moment's hesitation, Inspector Sugawa had settled into his own chair behind his desk. "Yes. It will be two years in July." He was a painfully thin man, with a look of frail delicacy about him, but his eyes were large and his gaze penetrating. It struck Otani that the uniform he wore looked wildly inappropriate on him, and that he would look much more seemly in the rich purple brocades of the formal vestments of a Buddhist abbot, seated under the shade of a ceremonial parasol as mountain priests in their weird garb of baggy leggings, short checked tunics and pill-box hats blew on their conch-shells as part of some festive ritual at a temple high in the Yoshino mountains.

"A curious sort of job you must have here. Not a great deal of trouble, I imagine."

"No, not really, sir. A lot of the people who live in Takarazuka commute to Osaka or Kobe to work. In that respect it's quiet enough. The majority of the people who come to the theatre are women and girls, and the Family Land amusement park tends to attract families with young children."

"Yes. It would."

"We tend to keep a rather careful eye on middle-aged or elderly men who wander about on their own. They sometimes make themselves objectionable to young girls."

"Ah. I can imagine." Otani rubbed his nose before going on. "I'm really on my way to Arima Onsen," he said then. "In connection with the death of a foreigner there last week. I'm quite interested to know how long it takes to drive from here to Arima by car. The bus takes about twenty-five minutes or so, I believe."

Normally in Otani's experience others were inclined to be loquacious in his presence, as though feeling some obscure need to justify their existence to him. With Inspector Sugawa he found the tables turned and was uneasily conscious of the great luminous eyes fixed on him and the immobility of the slender man on the other side of the desk.

"It isn't a journey I've had occasion to make myself very often," Sugawa said. "But it certainly isn't far. Eleven or twelve kilometres perhaps?"

Otani nodded. "If that."

"Well, even allowing for the twisting mountain road one ought to be able to get there easily in a quarter of an hour at this time of the year. Less, very probably."

"I would think so too. Anyway, I shall find out for myself before long. Tell me, Inspector, do you have much personal contact with the Takarazuka Theatre people?"

A faint smile flitted over Sugawa's thin face. "The Takarazuka Family Land, including the theatre, is the biggest enterprise in the town, sir. To all intents and purposes, it *is* the town. Seventy years ago this was a sleepy little hot-spring resort that nobody outside the Kobe area had ever heard of. It might have rated a single resident policeman, I suppose. It's true that most police activity associated with Takarazuka nowadays takes the form of traffic control, but even so we

127

maintain close liaison with the management, and I drop in there at least twice a month. They take in enormous sums of money in cash, as you can imagine. So security is a continuing concern."

Otani felt as if he had been rebuked. "Yes, of course. Silly of me not to have thought of that for myself. What about the actresses themselves, though? Any dealings with them?"

This time Sugawa's smile was quite broad. "I could answer you much more helpfully, Superintendent, if you would explain a little more clearly exactly what it is you want to know, and about whom. There are a great many more people in the theatre over there across the bridge than just management staff and actresses. There's a sizeable orchestra of about three dozen musicians, for example. Then there are set designers and stage-hands, electricians, costume staff, wig-makers, cooks, waitresses, cleaners and so forth. . ." He raised a slender hand expressively as his voice died away, and Otani coughed in some embarrassment.

"I'm sorry, Inspector. I owe you an apology. The fact is that I'm just feeling my way at this stage, and I'm afraid I have a very bad habit of keeping my colleagues in the dark while I sort out my own ideas."

Sugawa gestured again with his hand, this time depreciatingly. "Please don't think me presumptuous, sir. But I do in fact have a number of useful contacts over at the theatre. If there is any specific way in which I can be of assistance. . ."

Otani realised that he had been beating about the bush quite long enough, and sat up straighter in his chair. The movement also helped him to shake off the sense of falling into a kind of hypnotic trance under Sugawa's steady gaze. "Yes. Right. What do you know about Sachiko Chiba?"

Sugawa rose to his feet and moved towards the filing cabinet with the tiny pine tree in its simple brown-glazed ceramic bowl on top. The room was so small that he needed to take only a single sideways step to reach it and open the top drawer, from the front of which he took out a manila folder. He then sat down again at his desk and opened it.

128

"Miss Chiba. Still a popular star although she appears only rarely these days. You may be surprised to see that I have a small file on her. I have similar files on perhaps a dozen or so other Takarazuka stars. Not all of them, though. It's an odd thing that a few of them – invariably those who play male roles – attract not only the usual fan club letters that arrive in their hundreds every week, but also a less agreeable kind of communication. The Takarazuka public relations staff deal with all the usual fan-mail, of course. Send off signed photographs and so forth." Sugawa riffled through some of the loose sheets in the folder, then looked across again at Otani.

"I've been shown samples of letters from lovesick women of all ages, a good many housewives but mostly schoolgirls. Even some of what the Takarazuka staff think of as 'ordinary' letters are quite startlingly . . . frank, I suppose one might say."

Otani nodded. "It doesn't surprise me. You ought to glance at one or two of the comic magazines intended for junior high-school girls some time. But go on. I presume the staff pass over any objectionable ones to you to look into?"

"Precisely."

"And are the actresses to whom they are addressed aware of this practice?" Otani was more than a little shocked. "It is a criminal offence to open a letter addressed to another person without permission."

Sugawa coughed delicately. "Yes, Superintendent. I think I may safely say that all concerned are aware of the fact. All performing members of the company give their formal agreement under the terms of their contracts for mail addressed to them at the theatre to be opened, sorted and dealt with by the secretarial staff of the public relations department. Genuinely personal mail is usually quite easily identifiable, and in any case the girls who become stars rarely continue to live in the Takarazuka dormitories and can easily enough make their private addresses known to their friends."

Sugawa smiled again. "Even the vainest among them

129

hardly want to sit for an hour or so a day opening envelopes and reading starry-eyed requests for photographs and auto-graphs or listening to cassette tapes made by aspiring singers. My impression is that the services of the PR staff are warmly appreciated, and that the girls who handle the incoming mail soon develop an instinct as to which letters ought to be shown to the actresses they're addressed to. In such cases I believe they quite often draft replies for approval. It used to be a tedious process when everything had to be done by hand, but of course they've had word-processors for several years now. Incidentally, sir –"

Otani raised a hand to interrupt him. "I know what you're going to say, and I'm afraid the answer is, not yet. The finance committee of the prefectural government are dragging their feet over allocating adequate funds for the computerisation programme. I'm afraid you won't be getting a micro in this division for two or three years yet. I'm sorry."

Sugawa did not seem unduly cast down, and Otani suspected that neither of them would have the slightest idea what to do with a micro-computer if confronted with one. "Let's go back to this fan-mail business. As I now understand it, the actresses authorise the PR department to open their incoming mail, sort it and deal with it at their discretion, which discretion includes deciding which letters the address-ees will or will not see and perhaps reply to personally. Right?"

"That is so, yes."

"Now, in the case of some of them, objectionable letters are found among the incoming mail, and are referred to you here for investigation. Objectionable in what sense? I take it you mean obscene?"

"Yes. Most such letters are in fact obscene, but in addition some of them contain threats or amount to crude attempts to blackmail. Much of the material that comes our way represents relatively harmless fantasising, though it would most probably disgust and distress the addressees were they to see it. In this sense, what we and the PR staff are doing is

130

analogous to intercepting obscene telephone calls. Some material in fact arrives in the form of cassette tape recordings. Sometimes we can identify the originator and do something about it – there are a number of people known to us in this context, needless to say. All men, of course. A lot of the regular fan-mail from women and girls is as I have indicated highly erotic, but it's quite different from the truly obscene stuff I'm talking about now. Mostly we have to just note it and see if any pattern develops."

"And the threatening letters? And blackmail? It's difficult to see how one can blackmail a popular actress." Otani was puzzled.

"Let me just deal with the threats first. Most are of course inextricably linked with the obscenity and are again just so much fantasy, going into lurid detail about what the writer intends to do, or of course to be more accurate imagines he would like to do to the recipient. These are not taken seriously. Some on the other hand are obviously from really disturbed, even psychotic people who conceive what often comes across as a genuinely murderous hatred for particular women in the company, and when we come across a threat of acid-throwing or knifing we take it very seriously indeed. It's hard to be sure, of course, but I like to believe that officers assigned here have headed off one or two potentially horrifying attacks over the years."

"Depressing that a place with such a glamorous image should attract such attention." Otani reflected that he would not be telling Hanae about this particular conversation, and found himself belatedly approving of what he had earlier thought of as an unwarrantable censorship of the actresses' mail.

Sugawa looked again through the papers in the folder before him. "You asked about blackmail, sir. Well, curiously enough that brings us to Miss Chiba. That's not her real name, by the way."

"I never supposed it was. For people of my age there will only ever be one Sachiko Chiba. She and Takako Irie were the pin-up girls of my boyhood. . .forgive me, Inspector, this is no time for day-dreaming." In some embarrassment Otani fumbled for a cigarette; then abandoned the idea as he realised that there was no ashtray to be seen in the room and that Sugawa had not smoked throughout their quite lengthy conversation.

"Miss Chiba is, as I said earlier, still very popular, although she's in her thirties and concentrating more and more on teaching nowadays. I'm told she still gets a lot of fan-mail. In the past she used to have the occasional obscene letter addressed to her, but more recently just such a blackmail attempt has been made. You asked a moment ago how an actress could be vulnerable, sir. Well, it's all a question of image, really. Some of the women who play male roles are, well, perhaps a bit ambiguous in their private lives too, but most are perfectly normal and have sexual relationships with men. All the same, for professional reasons they keep very quiet about them, and the sensational magazines usually play along for their own reasons. Insinuations of lesbianism sell even more copies than straightforward 'Sex Lives of the Stars' revelations."

Otani was following Sugawa's reasoning with some difficulty, the more so because the Inspector's words were so much in contrast to his ascetic appearance.

"The official Takarazuka line is of course that their shows are healthy family entertainment, romantic but in no way sexy, and that's perfectly true, of course. Yet a lot of quite ordinary members of the public assume that the male role actresses are lesbians, and that they seduce all the young girls who join the company. Even though it's to a considerable extent a myth it's one that doesn't do any harm at the box office, and Takarazuka publicity doesn't exactly go out of its way to explode it." There was the ghost of a smile on Sugawa's face as he paused and sat back.

Otani nodded thoughtfully, feeling rather naive. "Yes. I see what you mean," he said, and waited for more as Sugawa again leafed through the papers in his file.

132

"Yes. Now in fact Miss Chiba has been secretly married and divorced twice, and has it seems had a number of heterosexual affairs. Yet her carefully contrived stage image is that of a masterful lesbian. Our potential blackmailer somehow got hold of some photographs of Sachiko Chiba engaged in unmistakeable heterosexual activities, and . . . well, sir, I need hardly go on. There are magazines that would certainly not object to paying a lot for such pictures and printing them trimmed just enough to keep clear of the pornography laws along with a sensational story which would to say the least greatly embarrass both Miss Chiba herself and the Takarazuka management."

"I see. Well, don't keep me in suspense, Inspector. How long ago did this happen, and how was it resolved?"

For the first time since Otani had arrived at the police station Inspector Sugawa looked somewhat ill at ease. "The first letter was intercepted about three weeks ago, sir. I should explain that the matter is not, in fact, yet resolved. That is why I was able to put my hands on the folder containing the relevant papers right away."

Chapter XVIII

"Of course, I suspected him from the first," Kimura said with a forced attempt at airiness, and then subsided into his chair as he noticed the expression on Otani's face. "What I mean to say is, when I first talked to him at the Oriental Hotel I was convinced that he knew a lot more than he was letting on." Otani was feeling rather tired, and experienced only a brief flicker of temptation to bait Kimura. Besides, in spite of his characteristically cocky remark Kimura still struck Otani as being curiously subdued, a couple of days after he had first noticed his changed manner.

"No doubt. But what we now know, thanks to Ninja, is that Ghafoor Khan is the man who phoned the workshop foreman at the taxi firm and arranged for the cab that killed Abdalla to be available at the material time. What we also know is that as matters stand it will be impossible to prove it. There is of course the further question – who actually drove it? Not Khan himself, because he was on foot in the vicinity and indeed was the one who identified Abdalla, isn't that right?"

He turned to Hara, who was leafing through a sheaf of notes. When arriving at Otani's office for the meeting he had been carrying in addition a pile of substantial books, which now reposed on the cracked brown linoleum near his chair. It was a second or two before he realised that he was being addressed, but then he blinked round at the other three men and nodded vigorously. "Yes, sir. That is so."

Otani sighed. "It really is rather depressing. No sooner do we manage to track somebody down than we find ourselves looking for somebody else."

"Feel his collar," Noguchi suggested. "I'll talk to him if you like."

Otani shook his head slowly. He preferred not to think about the ways in which Noguchi might have obtained the information that Ghafoor Khan had not only "booked" the cab but had for some years been dealing through the agency of the same go-between in stolen goods, mainly foodstuffs and textiles, and certainly had no intention of inviting him to question the Pakistani. When the time came he would do that himself, with or without Kimura's assistance, but certainly not with Noguchi's. "It's an idea, Ninja, but I think it might be more productive to leave him off guard for the moment."

Kimura uttered a strangled sound and Otani turned to him politely.

"Yes?"

"I'm sorry, but I'm afraid I have to say that it's inconceivable that Khan could be off guard after what you said to him in this office." Kimura's face was red with embarrassment but he went on gamely. "He now knows for sure that we're looking at him very closely indeed. I agree with Ninja. We have quite enough on him to pull him in, and if we don't he could give us the slip." Otani looked at him thoughtfully but said nothing, and the silence dragged on until Hara coughed deferentially.

"It's a very tentative hypothesis, but I should like to refer to the original report submitted by Woman Detective Migishima. I have a copy with me. In it she described a few of

135

the members of the congregation at the mosque who left before Abdalla and, needless to say, before the incident. If I may summarise the relevant passage, sir?" Otani nodded.

"Thank you. She refers to five persons in all, two of them elderly and *prima facie* unlikely to be of interest in this context. A third is described as being considerably younger, and dressed in flashy, ostentatious clothes. This is of course in itself suggestive, but then Officer Migishima continues as follows: 'Two young men then came out of the mosque. They looked like students, and appeared to be in a hurry, pushing their way past others. After going out of the gate they turned in the opposite direction to Tor Road and walked away quickly.' Highly significant, I would venture to suggest, sir."

Kimura's implied criticism of the way in which he had conducted the interview with Khan had given Otani pause: it was almost unheard of for him to speak in such a way. Hara's contribution made him feel much livelier, though, and he turned to Kimura in a friendly way.

"Her husband was with her that day, wasn't he?"

Kimura nodded. "Yes. He mentioned the incident to me first that evening when we were up at Arima."

"Splendid. Thank you for bringing up the matter, Hara. I should have remembered Officer Migishima's report myself. So either or both of these officers ought to be able to identify those men if they were to see them again." Then his shoulders slumped a little. "That's the problem, of course. We'll have photographs on file if they're resident in this area, but we're no further forward if they aren't. Then again, I don't have a great deal of faith anyway in photographic identification."

Another silence fell after Otani finished speaking, and he looked from one to another of his colleagues with his eyebrows raised in a mute appeal for help. None was forthcoming for some time, but eventually Noguchi shifted slightly in his chair, obviously about to say something. They all looked at him. "Got to start somewhere. Have the pair of them back there this Friday. See if they can spot them again. Might get lucky."

136

"Right!" Kimura said eagerly. Noguchi's terse suggestion seemed to have jerked him out of his lethargy again. "And in the meantime they can have a good look through the local aliens' files. We've sorted out all the Moslems anyway and put them on one side, so it won't take long."

"All right. I agree it's a start, but it's still a very long shot. Even if we can locate these three men again – or at least the two whose behaviour could give rise to suspicion – it's pure surmise that one of them drove that taxi. Hara, you'd better have somebody establish some precise timings. You know, how long it would take to walk quickly from the mosque to where the taxi was parked, get it started and drive back to the mosque, that sort of thing. We don't want to start pulling in people who might well be totally uninvolved, even if the Migishimas do manage to spot them again."

Otani looked at Noguchi. "I'm very grateful to you, Ninja. You've given this investigation a real boost. And sooner or later we'll have Khan in again and lean on him. Before we do that, though, we really do need at the very least some sort of theory of our own about motive, if only to help us decide on the best way to tackle him. I realise in retrospect that I probably handled him unwisely when I saw him."

He turned his gaze on the other two. Kimura was gazing at the ceiling, touched and embarrassed by the olive branch Otani had extended to him, while Hara's facial muscles were working as though he was trying to dislodge a fly from his nose while deprived of the use of his hands. Neither spoke, so Otani went on thinking aloud.

"In view of what Ninja discovered about Khan's relationship with his contact we must take it as certain that it *was* Khan who arranged to have the use of the taxi that day. There is objective scientific evidence that it was the vehicle which killed Abdalla, and in view of the timing and other circumstances it would be an affront to common-sense to doubt that the intention was to kill or at least seriously injure him. More likely the former. Agreed?" Hara nodded solemnly and Kimura with an air of impatience, while Noguchi appeared to

137

be deep in slumber.

"Right. Now why did Khan want Abdalla killed? Then there's a related question. Why did he choose a method which he must have hoped would lead us at least and possibly others to conclude that the death had been accidental? We all know that drivers in most of the hit-and-run cases we clear up turn out to have been drunk or something and simply scared of the consequences of an accident, not murderers or hit-men with contracts. Khan possibly counted on our interpreting this case like that. May even have worked out a contingency plan to support the idea if the driver had been caught."

Noguchi opened an eye and snorted. "He'd have had a job. Wouldn't have fooled anyone for a minute."

"With respect, sir, I agree with Inspector Noguchi." It was Hara. "The method selected undoubtedly involved very high risks for the driver, assuming as we must that he was a foreigner. A Japanese driver might if apprehended have feigned drunkenness – it is a simple matter to sprinkle sake or spirits on one's clothing. And could perhaps have said that he had stolen the unattended cab to go joy-riding."

"Well, why shouldn't Khan have hired a Japanese to do the job? He obviously has his connections." Kimura looked distinctly put out: Hara was making the kind of contribution he normally prided himself on.

"I have a different theory, sir," Hara continued, reaching down for one of the books on the floor beside him. "Based on the ambiguities which have already emerged concerning the *bona fides* of the victim, Abdalla, and especially the reaction of the Sudanese Embassy to the news of his death."

"Oh? And what is your theory?"

"Briefly, sir, I suggest that if things had not gone so satisfactorily from his point of view and the driver of the taxi *had* been stopped and questioned he would have committed suicide."

Kimura opened his mouth to speak but then thought better of it, and it was Otani who was the first to break the silence which followed Hara's bombshell. "What an extraordinary suggestion, Hara. Perhaps you'd care to enlighten us?" Hara had marked several places in the book he now held with slips of paper, and they all waited in patience as he found the one he wanted.

"I have been devoting some time to reading up on the political and religious tensions within the world of Islam, sir. In particular, I have found out what I could with the assistance of a friend of mine at Nagasaki University about the various organisations of extremists within the world. Many of them are small, and little is known about them. Others, like the so-called Muslim Brotherhood for example, are of long standing and highly influential, with supporters and agents in many countries, by no means all of them in the Middle East. I think it possible that Abdalla was not the innocent research scientist he claimed to be, but that he was an agent of the Sudanese regime, which has itself in recent years been adopting a markedly more fundamentalist stance, while still in uncomfortable alliance with the more moderate Egyptians. I think it possible that Abdalla was sent to Japan and to this area in order to spy upon certain Moslems here, that his true identity was discovered and that his assassination was decided upon."

"All right," Otani said dubiously. "I think I can follow you so far. But why should the fellow who killed Abdalla commit suicide if he'd been caught?"

"If my hypothesis is tenable, sir, the man who drove the car must have been a Moslem extremist. It is a tenet of Islam that the soul of one who dies in the course of doing God's work goes straight to Paradise. Martyrdom is not only envisaged but sometimes eagerly sought by such believers. They will never submit themselves to questioning provided the means of suicide is to hand."

"I see. So I presume that you agree with the others that we should bring in this Pakistani, Ghafoor Khan?" Hara twisted in his chair and appeared to be trying to wrap one leg round the other, but nodded.

"Yes, sir. I do."

"And do you *really* think that he might try to kill himself rather than answer our questions? He struck me as a reasonable, intelligent sort of man, even if he is obviously involved in all this up to the neck."

"If he suspects that we have firm evidence of his complicity, sir, yes."

Kimura had begun to splutter slightly in protest, and objected as soon as Hara paused to draw breath. "Muslim Brotherhood? Extremist? I never heard of anything so preposterous! Why, you haven't even met the man! The Superintendent and I have. He tried to sell me a suit, for goodness' sake. Granted he's a crooked businessman, granted Ninja seems to have established that he fixed up that taxi arrangement, but all this political and religious stuff is pure fantasy. Yes, I think we should pull him in before he does a disappearing act, but this suicide idea is absurd. The man must have had some personal grudge against Abdalla, that's all. Perhaps they were involved in some deal and Abdalla double-crossed him. That's reason enough for him to want to make it look like an accident."

Otani looked at Kimura in some surprise. "And it's just coincidence that Khan walked in here the other day with a suicide letter from the other one? Fuhaid? Come now, I seem to remember that it was you who put the idea of religious or political motivation into our minds in the first place, Kimura-kun. I agree that Hara's theory sounds a bit far-fetched, but it suggests a more credible motive than what you call 'a personal grudge'. Anyway, we're a very long way away from being able to feel confident about any line of thinking at the moment, and the more ideas any of you can come up with the better. The one concrete suggestion to have emerged so far is that the Migishimas should keep an unobtrusive watch on Friday on the men who come and go at the mosque. It's an excellent idea, and I'd like the arrangements to be made. If the men do turn up again, they must be required to give an account of their movements immediately after the last prayer meeting and those accounts must be checked very carefully indeed.

140

Oh, and let me remind you about the business of establishing timings." He hesitated, then turned to Kimura, concern in his eyes. "Kimura-kun. How are you feeling today? You didn't seem very well last time we met."

"Me? I'm fine, Chief. No problems."

"If you say so. Well, foreigners are your speciality. Do what you can to find out about Khan's personal background, but be scrupulously careful not to alert him. You can have a word with the Foreign Office liaison staff or even your CIA friend at the American Consulate General if you're careful about it, but leave the gangster contacts to Ninja. By the way, I've already spoken to Ambassador Atsugi and asked him to find out what he can about Abdalla. But let's keep Hara's theory to ourselves for the moment."

He stretched and then looked at his watch. "Time's getting on, but before we break up I want to turn to the Arima business briefly. I had a useful talk to Inspector Sugawa at Takarazuka yesterday, about this woman who calls herself Sachiko Chiba. Then I went on to Arima and finally managed to talk to the receptionist girl who's been so hard to get hold of. Let me tell you about Sachiko Chiba first, though. . ."

Chapter XIX

The small apartment block in which Shulamit Steiner's flat was located was similar to a great many others in the mixed area between Sannomiya and New Kobe Station above the city where the so-called "bullet" trains stopped. Although four storeys high, it was no wider or deeper than an ordinary house or shop, and the ground floor indeed consisted of a sushi bar called "Mon". A narrow door at the side gave access to a vinyl-tiled miniature lobby with a bank of six mailboxes fixed to the wall, and then almost at once to a precipitous staircase which led to the six minuscule flats, two on each floor.

The approach to Apartment 402 on the top floor had become quite familiar to Kimura over the past few months, but he had never met any of the other tenants of the building; only heard the muffled sound coming from their TV sets or radios and smelt the pungent aroma of soy sauce or pickles as he passed on his way to or from a session with Shulamit.

There was nobody about at the dead hour of three-thirty in

142

the afternoon and he was confident of not being caught by Shulamit herself. She had telephoned him at his own apartment early that morning to cry off their lunch date, explaining that she planned to spend the whole afternoon at Takarazuka, going there straight from the university library. It was just as well. The bombshell of Otani's account of his conversation with the inspector at the Takarazuka police station had left Kimura in no state to face Shulamit again for the first time after the fiasco at his flat, and he needed time to pick his way through the shifting sands of suspicion and confusion in which he felt himself to be trapped.

The front door to Shulamit's flat, like those of the others, was of plain metal painted a dull green, and it had an ordinary cylinder lock. The crags and furrows of Noguchi's face had arranged themselves in an expression of surprise when Kimura asked to borrow a few skeleton keys for cylinder locks for a couple of hours but he had nodded and said nothing, either as he wandered off or when he returned a few minutes later and handed over the bunch which had been spoiling the line of Kimura's jacket ever since.

It had been many years since Kimura had last made an illicit entry into premises of any kind, and although it was a childishly simple matter to check the make of the lock and try the matching keys he found that his hand was trembling and that his forehead was wet with sweat when the first two he tried failed to operate the lock. He was lucky with the third key and sidled into the flat quickly as the door swung open, then closed the door quietly behind him and slipped out of his shoes as he stepped up from the entranceway.

He was already in the tiny kitchen, which boasted no more than a sink with a gas water heater mounted on the wall above, a store cupboard whose top constituted a constricted working surface and also accommodated a double gas cooking ring, and a miniature refrigerator. The door to the equally cramped bathroom was on his right and the all-purpose tatami-matted living-and-sleeping room ahead of him. Although Kimura had no idea what he was looking for, he consoled himself with the thought that it could hardly take very long to search the apartment.

He began with the piles of books and papers near the portable electric typewriter on the square table pushed to one side of the room, beside the window which admitted a little light but offered no view save that of a blank concrete wall about two metres away. There was a sliding screen of latticed wood and translucent shoji paper which could be used to conceal the dismal prospect in the evening.

The table and the single chair were of a kind often found in Japan with flat wooden runners joining the legs at the bottom to prevent their becoming embedded in the yielding tatami. As Kimura knew from pleasant personal experience, there was just room for Japanese-style bedding to be laid on the matting between the table on the one side of the room and the built-in store cupboards on the other, and Shulamit's radio-cassette recorder and a bedside lamp stood on the matting beside where it would go when she took it out of the cupboard at night. The phone was also on the floor, in the corner. A give-away calendar advertising Nikka Whisky hung on the wall opposite the door, and there were a couple of picture postcards fastened to the door-frame with drawing pins, along with an ornate object which Shulamit had told him was a mezuzah which really ought to be outside the front door. There was no other furniture.

Kimura glanced quickly at the books. Five of them were dictionaries, including one listing the Chinese characters used in written Japanese. There was also an English-Hebrew dictionary which he had noticed before and leafed through once or twice out of curiosity, and a fat paperback called *The Fontana Dictionary of Modern Thought*. Among the loose papers were leaflets announcing various Takarazuka productions, a tourist map of Kobe and a copy of the current Kobe University *Bulletin*, two letters in ripped-open envelopes bearing American stamps and Chicago postmarks, and a promotional leaflet for a new brand of shampoo. In the typewriter itself was a sheet of paper with half a dozen lines of

144

typing on it, and Kimura sat down to read them.

"was found that the original responses to the first (Mark
One) questionnaire led to problems in the cross-
referencing of the immediate and derived variables with
others such as inhibition, upbringing, age etc. which
suggested inadequate formulation of questions. It was
therefore redesigned to elicit activity ratings"

Kimura sighed. On the one hand it was difficult to imagine
that a murderer or an accessory to murder could sit and
solemnly compose such prose, and this was a relief. On the
other hand it made him feel intellectually inadequate.

There was a ring-binder file on the floor under the table and
he reached down for it and looked through the contents,
which appeared to consist of far, far more of the same kind of
thing. In a pocket at the back was a letter on University of
Chicago headed paper, apparently from Shulamit's academic
supervisor. He put the file back on the floor and turned his
attention to the letters on the table, for the first time
conscious of intrusion into her privacy. They were both from
the same person, obviously Shulamit's mother, and full of
banal family news.

Kimura returned the letters to their envelopes wishing he
had not read them. His own family relationships were
minimal, and for most of his adult life he had been
emotionally frugal, deriving huge enjoyment from sex but
preferring not to know too much about the personal lives of
the women with whom he had love affairs. He had never lived
with a woman and had no desire to: a night of sexual pleasure
was for him greatly enhanced by privacy before and after. He
took no pleasure in togetherness when it involved washing
dishes, dealing with laundry and cleaning up the bathroom,
and could not understand the majority of his acquaintances,
men and women alike, who professed to enjoy domesticity.

Kimura knew that Shulamit kept the futons and pillows
which made up her bedding with a few sheets and towels in

the left-hand side of the big cupboard which occupied the whole of the wall opposite the window, and her suitcases, clothes and other possessions in the other. With an audible sigh he went over and opened the right-hand sliding door. The modest collection of garments in the hanging space gave off Shulamit's characteristic perfume, as did the underwear in a shallow imitation lacquer tray on top of the set of four drawers which constituted the lower half of the cupboard. A large and a small suitcase were stowed on the deep shelf above the hanging space, and Kimura checked them first. They contained nothing except a small velvet bag with a silver bracelet and two pairs of earrings inside.

Then he looked through the drawers, starting with the bottom one. In this he found three pairs of shoes and a rather smart handbag with nothing in it except two crumpled paper handkerchiefs and a lipstick. The next one up yielded two carefully folded sweaters and three pairs of thick winter tights, and the third three blouses and a silk scarf on top of a few gramophone records featuring Takarazuka stars. Kimura noticed that their covers carried bold autographs done with a felt-tipped pen, and presumed that they were presents to Shulamit. Sachiko Chiba was not among those represented.

He opened the top drawer. There was not a lot in it, and what there was consisted largely of miscellaneous stationery, ball-point pens, spare typewriter ribbons, a bottle of Sno-pake and a box of Tippex correction films. There was also a paper wallet of the kind developed photographs are returned in: this one advertised Fuji film. Kimura lifted it out of the drawer carefully and opened it. Most of the prints inside were recent, showing Shulamit against identifiably Japanese backgrounds and often with Japanese companions, including Sachiko Chiba and others who were obviously also members of the Takarazuka company.

The remaining photographs were older. There was one of a middle-aged couple, presumably her parents, and Kimura found himself wondering if in twenty-five years' time Shulamit would look like her mother and hoping for her sake that she would not. Another showed Shulamit herself in what looked like academic surroundings, a university campus perhaps. The sun was shining, but she was wearing a winter coat and smiling up at the tall man at her side, who was looking down at her with an expression of tenderness. They were holding hands. The same man was shown alone in another print, posed rather self-consciously at a desk with an enormous tome open in front of him and against a background of laden bookshelves.

There were two more pictures, showing a very much younger Shulamit wearing shorts and a T-shirt on a beach, her fiery hair contrasting strikingly with the silvery sand at her bare feet and the vivid blues of the sea and the cloudless sky behind her. In one of them she was alone, and in the other with another woman and a man in similar beach clothes in a laughing group, their arms resting on each others' shoulders as they faced the photographer.

Kimura stood as though turned to stone, becoming aware of the sound of traffic outside which seemed to emphasise the utter stillness inside the poky little flat, and with the faint suggestion of Shulamit's perfume in his nostrils. It was true, then. And the truth more startling than he had imagined even in his wildest flights of fancy. Eventually he bestirred himself and went over to the window where the light was better. There he again gazed at the photograph in fascination for a long time. Then he carefully put the print in his own wallet before replacing the others in the paper folder and restoring it to its place in the drawer, which he closed with exaggerated care.

It was by any reckoning a highly significant find, and if he could believe his eyes, a shattering one. Kimura had no idea what to do next, beyond feeling an urgent desire to get away from the flat and try to order his thoughts before reporting to Otani, who would have to be told as a matter of urgency.

He took a last, sad look round the little apartment which had been the scene of many fiercely exciting moments. He did not find it particularly shabby; although he himself lived in much more comfortable surroundings, plenty of ordinary people including couples with babies had to pay good money to live in such places, and Shulamit was lucky to have it all to herself. He would never forget the good times in Apartment 402, but it was now inconceivable that he would ever be back.

He moved to the front door and eased his shoes on with the aid of the long-handled shoe-horn propped up in the corner, listening intently as he did so. There was nothing to be heard from outside, so he opened the door quietly and re-inserted the skeleton key in the outside of the lock to enable him to shut it again noiselessly after him, then stepped out.

He had almost closed the door again when the silence was shattered by the sound of Shulamit's telephone beginning to ring. It made him jump, and he fumbled over closing the door, producing a metallic boom. The ringing went on, although now muffled by the closed door, and Kimura found it peculiarly unnerving. So much so that he tripped at the top of the staircase and fell headlong down the first flight, his head violently striking first the metal handrail and then the wall below.

He had no idea when he came to how long he had been unconscious. Such considerations were insignificant compared with the agonising pain in his right foot and ankle, which were twisted under him, the excruciating throbbing in his head, and the shock of seeing Shulamit's face looming over him in the semi-darkness of the ill-lit staircase.

"You okay, Jiro? Broken anything?" He could manage only an incoherent groan by way of reply. "Think you can make it up to the apartment? Come on, now." The voice, he thought, sounded less concerned than it should, and as he began to crawl painfully up the stairs after her he felt monstrously ill-used. Her next remark was even less encouraging.

"Don't worry, I picked up the skeleton keys you dropped, Jiro. We'll just see how badly hurt you are, then you can tell me whether you were coming or going. Okay?"

Chapter XX

"Want me to come up with you?"

Kimura nodded. "Please. If you have time." His head was still sore and painful, but the elastic bandage which now immobilised his ankle and the light aluminium crutches which they had lent him at the private surgical clinic not far from Shulamit's apartment made it possible for him to get about without too much discomfort.

She went into the lift first and held the doors open for him as he hobbled in. "Lucky you live in a classy place like this with an elevator," she said.

They had hardly spoken during the past hour or so. The first-aid facilities at Shulamit's flat were minimal, but she had bathed the cut on Kimura's head with cold water and used one of the woollen tights he had seen earlier in the drawer of her cupboard to improvise temporary strapping for his ankle, which by the time Kimura had hauled himself back up the stairs had swollen grotesquely and was obviously badly sprained, if not broken.

Shulamit's expression throughout had been grim and set and Kimura for his part had been almost glad of the pain, which absolved him from the necessity to talk much. She handed him the bunch of skeleton keys without a word and did not repeat her question about whether he had been coming from or going to her flat when he fell.

It was Shulamit who had suggested taking him to the nearby Ueda Clinic, one of the small but efficient if costly private enterprise hospitals which abound in Japan, and who went ahead to find a taxi while Kimura negotiated the stairs once more by the expedient of sitting down and taking them one by one on his backside. At the Ueda Clinic X-rays had shown no fracture, and the cut on his head needed only two stitches. While his injuries were being attended to Kimura's thoughts about Shulamit had toppled chaotically about his mind, but his reaction on emerging from the treatment room and finding her waiting for him in the lobby had been one of pleasure and gratitude. Only during the silent taxi ride to his apartment had the confusion and anger begun to take over again.

Once inside his flat he looked at her long and hard. The great eyes that stared back at him were cold and bitter. "Would you like a drink?" he asked.

"Yes. Sit down. I'll fix them." Shulamit knew her way about the flat and went into the kitchen as Kimura lowered himself into the armchair, then quickly took the photograph from his wallet and slipped it well out of sight underneath the chair-cushion.

Shulamit returned and handed him a glass of whisky and water with a hand which trembled slightly. He noticed that her own drink was perceptibly darker in colour than the one she had mixed for him. "Cheers," he said solemnly, and she nodded gravely in response before drinking deeply, her eyes never leaving his. "Won't you sit down?"

Shulamit was wearing jeans and her usual sweatshirt, and she sank down gracefully and sat cross-legged on the carpet some distance away from him, her back propped against the

150

frame of the door leading to the bedroom. "Why didn't you tell me you knew her long ago? In Israel?" he asked quietly. Her eyes widened momentarily, but there was no other change in her expression, and she said nothing.

"It's gone too far for silence, Shulamit," he went on. "We know a great deal now. We shall find out the rest. I shall probably have to hand over my part in the investigation to a colleague . . . my feelings for you have been getting badly in the way. Unless you'll help me to help you."

Shulamit still said nothing, but drained her glass and stood up. Kimura thought she was going to leave, but instead she went into the kitchen and made herself another drink, and then returned to her former position without a word. Kimura looked at her sadly. He found her in her vulnerability more attractive than ever. "I'll tell you just some of what we know, and I'll begin by pointing out that you prepared your alibi too carefully. People often do that." He took out his wallet again and this time took from it the Dai-ichi Bank cashpoint withdrawal slip which Shulamit had tossed towards him in the same room a couple of nights previously. "You didn't even look at it before you told me it was timed one thirty-eight. You were quite right, though. So it is. People going casually to the bank to get some money don't note the time and remember it so exactly, Shulamit. You didn't in fact go to the bank last Friday at all. You couldn't have done, because you were at the Grand View Hotel in Arima, covering for Fuhaid. Weren't you?"

"You're out of your mind." There was an odd kind of serenity about Shulamit's pose as she sat there so neatly with her slender legs crossed, glass in one hand while the other rested lightly on her thigh. Something about her contained immobility reminded Kimura of the images of the Buddhist bodhisattva Jizo, that kindly and merciful protector of the souls of children in hell, and to his own astonishment he felt the beginning of tears pricking at his eyes. It was with a fierce effort of will that he managed to maintain his carefully matter-of-fact manner.

151

"Perhaps you don't realise that most banks have concealed video cameras covering their cashpoints and keep the tapes for quite some time." Shulamit caught her breath for only a fraction of a second, but it was enough. Kimura had not yet been in touch with the bank and had no idea whether or not video-tapes were in fact preserved for any length of time. It was something which would have to be checked sooner or later, but his bluff had paid off anyway.

"Don't bother to deny it, Shulamit. You were at Arima. Because Sachiko Chiba is very close to you, and has been ever since you met her on the kibbutz. You were still a teenager – no, don't interrupt, we already know the dates she was there, and I'm guessing that you went during a summer vacation, or even a whole year before you began at Chicago University. It will be the simplest thing in the world to check, I assure you." He drank some more of the whisky. As the alcohol was entering his bloodstream it was making his bruises and the stitches in his head throb more painfully, but it helped all the same.

"It might very well have been Sachiko Chiba who first sparked off your interest in Japan, but however that may be, you kept in close touch after you returned to America. Very possibly saw each other again. There or in Israel. When she wrote a couple of years later to say she was returning to Japan and hoping to re-join the Takarazuka company you conceived the idea of coming here to do your graduate work. I don't doubt for a moment that you had to make formal contact with the Takarazuka people in the roundabout way you described to me, but you knew that it was a foregone conclusion that Sachiko would be able to fix things so that she would be assigned to help you with your research. Everything started off splendidly, until you found out she was in trouble, because Fuhaid was in Japan. Then you felt obligated to do your best to help her."

Kimura clumsily eased himself forward in his chair until he was able to drop to his knees. Then he shuffled forward until he was close to Shulamit, and taking the glass from her hand

152

set it down carefully. She made no attempt to resist him then or when he propped himself against the wall at her side and put his arms round her shoulders, drawing her to him. Then all at once she clutched at him and buried her face in his shoulder, quivering and shaking as she sobbed. "I care about you, Shulamit," he said gently. "I don't want to believe that you killed Fuhaid. In fact I don't believe it. I'm not sure yet whether or not you've committed any other crime. But I'm certain you were there at the hotel with him, and if I'm to help you I must know exactly what happened that day."

Shulamit gradually disentangled herself from his arms and sat up straight. Kimura watched as she clenched her fists and battled to bring her breathing under control. He began to fear that the doors he had forced at such cost were closing in his face, and knew that he had somehow to jam them open.

"Listen, Shulamit," he said harshly. "I know now that Fuhaid was really a Jew. You met him in Israel too. Was it Sachiko or you who had the affair with him there? Or both of you?"

Chapter XXI

"Thank you," Otani said fervently. "Thank you very much, Atsugi-san." He put the upstairs extension phone down and returned to the window from which he had been looking at the dark sweep of the bay beyond the illuminated ribbons of the highways linking Osaka and Kobe. It was beginning to be humid and visibility was not very good, but in his imagination he could see the prospect on a dry, sparkling winter night, extending from Wakayama Prefecture away to the left and round the whole of Osaka Bay to Awaji Island in the Inland Sea to his right.

He always enjoyed the few minutes before bed, while Hanae was still downstairs cleaning her teeth, and she was quite accustomed to coming up to find the room in darkness and her husband standing silently at the window. Usually he would turn as she entered the room and bend down to switch on the dim bedside lamp with its bamboo shade for her, but that night he stayed where he was and Hanae approached him from behind, resting her head lightly on his shoulder.

"You smell nice," he said absent-mindedly, and moved her round so that she stood beside him and he could slip one arm round her waist. "It's quite misty tonight. I think we may have more rain." Hanae stood there contentedly enough, sharing his dreamy mood and enjoying his familiar warmth.

"That was Ambassador Atsugi on the phone," he said after a while.

"Really? So late?"

"Yes. He wanted to pass on a message the Foreign Ministry have just received from our Embassy in the Sudan. It was something I'd asked him to check for me."

"You seem quite pleased about it, whatever it was."

"I suppose I am really. It answers some questions but on the other hand gives rise to more. You remember the evening Kimura came here and talked about the Sudanese scientist?"

"Of course."

"Well, it seems that the Dr el Abdalla who was killed in Kobe *was* bogus after all. There was an agricultural scientist of that name at the University of Khartoum until a few months ago, but he died suddenly of a heart attack. Atsugi has arranged for his people in Tokyo to check his application form and other papers with the scholarship foundation there. It's quite likely that they're perfectly genuine. I mean, that the real Abdalla had applied for and been awarded the scholarship and then somebody did some quick thinking when he died and substituted somebody else to come here."

Hanae shivered. "My feet are getting cold," she murmured. "Tell me the rest of it in bed." Otani smiled to himself, squeezed and then released her, stripping off his own yukata as he knelt and then slipped between the futons laid directly on the sweet-smelling tatami matting. Hanae always kept hers on in bed, and it was a continuing source of wonder to him that when she rose again in the morning it was hardly crumpled.

"But who?" she asked when she had settled herself to her satisfaction. "And why?"

"Good questions. You should have joined the police

155

yourself." Otani was lying flat on his back, his eyes wide open in the darkness. "So far as the 'who' part is concerned, Atsugi agrees with me that it's hard to see how such a substitution could have been worked except by the government, with the connivance of the university authorities in the Sudan. We can only infer that the phoney Abdalla was some kind of agent. When we were thinking about such a possibility the other day in my office somebody – Hara I think it was – suggested that for some reason the Sudanese must have wanted somebody in place down here in the Kansai to undertake a fairly long-term task. Otherwise they could much more easily have used one of their own diplomats in Tokyo. I mentioned to you that it's now pretty well established that he was killed deliberately?"

Hanae shivered again, but this time not because she was cold. "Yes. How awful."

"Well, we're pretty sure we know who organised the killing. And there's a link between him and the other man who died. At Arima Onsen."

"Oh. Did you find the woman you were looking for?"

"I think so." Otani rolled on to his side and propped himself on one elbow to look down at Hanae's face, pale and solemn in the moonlight from the open window. "I'd like to tell you about her. But it's very confidential, Ha-chan."

Hanae stiffened a little. "Of course. But if you'd rather not. . ."

Otani flopped back. "No, no, I know you won't mention it to anyone. I'm sorry. Well, I've been back a couple of times to Arima, and to Takarazuka. I needn't trouble you with the details, but the name of one of the Takarazuka actresses came up rather unexpectedly in connection with the Arima case. Sachiko Chiba."

"Sachiko Chiba? But she – "

"I know what you're going to say. I jumped to the same conclusion. But this is another Sachiko Chiba. I found out quite a lot about her. Firstly she is, or was up till very recently, being blackmailed. Secondly she has had a rather unorthodox career. She joined the company in the usual way as a young

156

girl and showed immediate promise, but just when she was beginning to make a big name for herself she was divorced, resigned and went abroad. To work in some sort of farming community in Israel. I was surprised to find that a lot of young Japanese did the same thing over the years between the fifties and the early seventies."

"I know. Mrs Kobayashi down at the rice shop has a niece who went there. She married an Israeli. A commercial artist, I think."

Hanae sounded quite blasé, but Otani was intrigued. "A commercial artist on a farm? That sounds a bit unlikely."

"Don't be silly. You know quite well what I mean."

Otani didn't, but carried on anyway. "Well, at all events this sort of volunteer work seems to have gone right out of fashion within the last ten years. I don't know how long most of these Japanese youngsters who went there reckoned to stay, but it seems that after two or three years of life in Israel Sachiko Chiba decided she'd made a big mistake and came back to Japan. What's more, she applied to rejoin Takarazuka, and although it's very much against their regular policies they thought so much of her that they made an exception in her case and took her back. It wasn't long before she was a star."

"It all sounds very complicated," Hanae murmured. It was obvious to Otani that she was becoming very drowsy. He waited for a minute or two before preparing to go on, but she said nothing more and her breathing had become very regular. Resignedly he abandoned the story and left her undisturbed.

Sleep in his case was far away, and he lay there quietly thinking again about his meeting with the impressive Inspector Sugawa at Takarazuka and his subsequent fifteen-minute drive to Arima and conversation with the receptionist at the Arima Grand View Hotel. The exact distance between the two towns proved to be a little over 10 kilometres and might have been covered more quickly, but Otani had instructed his driver Tomita to make good time without taking any risks. Fifteen minutes was about right for normal daytime traffic.

The long-awaited interview with the receptionist had been something of a disappointment. She was a bandy-legged girl with an eager manner who readily agreed with everything Otani suggested but volunteered almost nothing. It had taken all the skill born of his long experience as an interrogator to elicit from her that the woman who had accompanied Hossein Fuhaid to the hotel for the so-called "lunchtime course" had been wearing dark glasses and had long hair, and that she had behaved quite normally in the sense of hovering well in the background as ladies in such circumstances tended to do. The dark glasses were nothing unusual, either. She had been wearing a light spring coat, the girl thought she remembered; but couldn't be sure. It *was* distinctly out of the ordinary for a foreigner to patronise the hotel, after all, and the girl apologised for not having paid much attention to the lady. She had been concentrating on the gentleman, being somewhat embarrassed by the situation.

Otani had thanked her and let her go, then gratefully taken possession of the plastic shopping bag and its contents which the manageress had been keeping for him in a corner of her office since his urgent telephone call from the Portliner station on Port Island. The manageress was obviously pleased to have put Otani in her debt, and graciously confirmed the description of the coat and dark glasses worn by Fuhaid's companion.

After eating a late lunch of breaded pork cutlet and shredded raw cabbage with rice and miso soup alone, while his driver went off to forage for himself, Otani had returned to Takarazuka in a thoughtful mood. Sugawa had done what he asked and obtained a copy of the company call-sheet for the fatal Friday which he helpfully interpreted for Otani. It indicated that Sachiko Chiba had been involved in a rehearsal for the whole of the morning, and that she had been performing during the evening, in the show which began at 6.30. Otani had instructed Sugawa to make no attempt to seek confirmation of any alibi which might emerge, and he reassured Otani that the assistant stage-manager who had provided the call-sheet had no idea of the reason for the request. Otani then made another request, which Sugawa thought he could meet without too much trouble, but until hearing from him again Otani remained in a great muddle, with the identity of Fuhaid's companion still shrouded in mystery.

It could not have been Sachiko Chiba if she was rehearsing all the morning; yet she had been free of commitments in the afternoon. One thing seemed to be definite. There was hardly time for Fuhaid to have slipped out of the hotel unseen immediately after going with his woman companion to the room allotted to them, gone from Arima to Kobe, driven the car which had killed the mysterious Sudanese impostor and returned to the hotel in time to conduct his post-lunchtime negotiations with the manageress at the desk and then go out *again*, this time openly, in order to return at about four-thirty. Or might there have been?

He turned over restlessly on to his side, reached out and looked at the luminous dial of his wrist-watch which was lying on the tatami beside the bed. Eleven-thirty. He put the watch down again and was about to try to shut his mind down and go to sleep when a soft hand crept up his thigh and a moment later Hanae rolled over and nibbled at his left earlobe. The warmth of her breath in his ear at once began to have the effect it always did on him, and her inquisitive fingertips did the rest. "I thought you were asleep," he said happily as he untied the bow of her narrow sash and opened her yukata.

"I was, but now I'm awake again. You can tell me about your Takarazuka lady friend another time, though."

It was quiet in Kimura's flat. Shulamit was fast asleep, fully dressed on top of his bed, overcome by emotional exhaustion and alcohol. He sat at the table and put the finishing touches to his notes, then remembered to wind up his ingenious new watch. Looking at it he sighed. It was too late to disturb the

Old Man's slumbers. His report would have to wait till morning.

Inspector Jiro Kimura hauled himself over to the armchair again and tried to make himself comfortable. It was the first time in his life that he had ever had a woman lying on his bed and failed to join her there.

Chapter XXII

The vet who owned and ran the Dogs' Hospital opposite the mosque looked a little like the Pekinese he was cradling in his arms, for his hair was long and silky and his features small and somehow crumpled. On the other hand, his wispy beard gave him something also of the look of a television intellectual. He was a bustling, helpful soul, though, and made no objection when Junko Migishima showed him her credentials and requested his cooperation in allowing her to make use of an upper room as an observation post for an hour or so.

Indeed, once he fully grasped the fact that the attractive young woman with the delicious smile really was a police officer he became quite enthusiastic about the idea, and went on to speak at length and with some feeling about the inconvenience of having the mosque just across the street from his premises. The sound of chanting at dawn disturbed the dogs, and needless to say the frightful business of the traffic accident two weeks before had upset them out of all belief.

161

As he rambled on he seemed to be moving happily and with some rapidity to the conclusion that the police had it in mind to take proceedings which might lead to the closing down of the mosque altogether, and it was with difficulty that Junko managed at length to convince him that so far as her assignment was concerned, time was of the essence.

The vet having fallen into a conspiratorial silence, he handed the Pekinese over to his assistant, a plump girl in her late teens, and led Junko with many extravagant winks and beckonings through the waiting room and the surgery behind and up a staircase at the back, to a pleasantly furnished Western-style sitting-room which directly overlooked the mosque. There he left her with evident reluctance. The whole building was redolent of the smell of dog and antiseptic, but Junko soon became adjusted to it as she opened the capacious shoulder-bag she had brought with her and took from it a Nikon camera equipped with motor-drive and a walkie-talkie radio.

She had adjusted the focus and aperture to her satisfaction and was turning her attention to the radio when there was a timid tap at the door and the vet tip-toed in bearing a tray on which was a steaming cup of coffee and a substantial piece of strawberry shortcake on a plate.

"Oh. Thank you very much. You are very kind," she said in a normal conversational voice, at which he started in alarm and placed a finger over his lips as he nodded and smiled in the direction of the hissing and crackling radio. "It's all right," Junko said gently. "It's only receiving at the moment, not transmitting."

A look of disappointment spread over her host's face as he retreated to the open door, but Junko treated him to one of her most incandescent smiles and gave him a thumbs-up sign which he returned with vigour before disappearing again. Junko returned to her post at the window, prudently placing the tray within reach on the seat of a convenient chair, and took up the radio hoping as she did so that there would be at least one dog, and preferably several, in need of the vet's

162

professional services during the next hour.

Her husband was about a hundred yards away, his own radio concealed in a plastic-covered paper shopping bag. Migishima had been idling along the road stopping to examine the goods on display outside open-fronted shops and the plastic representations of various dishes in the windows of restaurants and coffee bars, and was currently leafing through one of an array of comic magazines in a rack outside one of the new "7-11" 24-hour grocery chain-stores which had been sprouting up all over Kobe in recent years. He wore a small speaker in one ear and hoped that passers-by would take it for a new design of Sony Walkman.

The Migishimas had decided between themselves that if Junko spotted any of the three men they were looking for on the way into the mosque they would take no immediate action, but would wait and intercept him or them on the way out. The patrolmen at the nearby police box had been alerted to respond at once if help was needed, but the plan was to avoid attracting attention through the involvement of uniformed officers if possible. What neither of the Migishimas knew was that the bulky workman in overalls supported comfortably by a broad canvas strap half-way up an electricity-supply pole where he was fiddling with a recalcitrant junction-box cover was Ninja Noguchi.

The tall double doors of the mosque were both open, and as Junko finished the last of her strawberry shortcake she saw the first few worshippers arrive in ones and twos; but she recognised none of them. She picked up the radio, pressed the transmit button and reported the fact succinctly to her husband and simultaneously to the police box in Tor Road and, unknowingly, to Noguchi on his perch.

Junko did recognise the emaciated man in the white cap of the *haji* but did not bother to report his arrival, nor that of Abdul Ghafoor Khan, whom she recognised not only from the photograph she had shown to the old woman neighbour of Hossein Fuhaid but also because seeing him again in context brought vividly back to her mind the horrifying recollection of

163

Khan standing near the crumpled body of Abdalla and speaking earnestly to a uniformed policeman as he identified the dead man. All at once she wished she hadn't eaten the strawberry shortcake, but managed to overcome the nausea which swept over her by concentrating on later arrivals.

It was the two young men who looked like students that she was trying hard to spot, and she almost missed the thick-set, thirtyish man who had worn the flared trousers and body-hugging flowered shirt on the previous occasion. This was partly because he was dressed this time in a lightweight suit, but fortunately he paused at the gate and turned to greet another man who had approached from the opposite direction, and Junko recognised his face and his curly hair. There was time to take two good shots of him with the Nikon before he disappeared inside and she made her report.

Although Junko took photographs of all the younger men among the arriving worshippers, and was fully alert to the probability that if the two others she was on the lookout for did turn up they would do so singly rather than together, she was disappointed: by twelve-forty she was fairly sure that neither of them had arrived. She reported the fact to Migishima and told him that she was on her way to join him, then put her radio and camera back in the holdall and made ready to leave. To extricate herself from the Dogs' Hospital proved to be almost as time-consuming as getting into it had been, but Junko eventually managed to escape by indicating the looming figure of her husband outside the door and explaining quite truthfully that she had urgent police business to discuss with her colleague outside.

Migishima was in a very twitchy state by the time she joined him and they crossed the road to take up a position close to the gate, for he was convinced that their quarry was about to escape. In fact they had over ten minutes to wait before the double doors were opened and the first of the congregation began to leave. This time the Migishimas made no attempt to conceal their interest in the men emerging from the gate, and attracted a number of hostile stares in return.

164

Abdul Ghafoor Khan was among the first dozen to leave the building, and he stopped short at the top of the steps when he saw the burly young Japanese and the girl at his side gazing up at him, hesitated and then went out through the gate slowly, pausing again a few yards away from them and waylaying an obvious acquaintance whom he engaged in conversation, his eyes repeatedly flicking towards the Migishimas.

About two minutes later the tough-looking younger man with the curly hair came down the steps and out through the gate. He turned in the direction opposite to that Khan had taken, and Migishima turned and followed him, closing up after he had walked about ten yards. "Sorry to bother you, sir," he said in Japanese. "I am a police officer. Do you speak Japanese?"

The man stopped and looked Migishima up and down. "I understand a little Japanese," he replied. "What is all this about?"

Migishima took out his warrant card and showed it to him. "It's in connection with the accident which took place here last Friday," he was beginning, when a thin hand gripped his arm with surprising force.

"Who are you? What do you want?" It was Khan, seemingly in an agitated state.

Migishima shook him off irritatedly. "I am a police officer," he intoned again, trying to disregard Khan, who had turned to the other man and was talking to him rapidly in a language Migishima could not begin to identify. At this point they were joined by Junko, whose clear voice cut through the hubbub.

"You are Abdul Ghafoor Khan, and you are impeding a police officer in the execution of his duties," she announced firmly, at which the Pakistani turned and gaped at her. "I am also a police officer and we require both of you to accompany us to the police box to answer some questions."

Khan looked around wildly and then again spoke with great urgency to the man in the lightweight suit while pointing as though indicating a location. The language he used was unintelligible to the Migishimas. A tense silence followed, lasting less than a second but seeming much longer, after which both men suddenly sprinted off. Junko was after them instantly, and caught and tackled the younger man, whose face registered blank amazement as he found himself on the ground without having the least idea how he had arrived there. Meantime Khan cannoned into the waiting bulk of Ninja Noguchi, who winced and grunted as he seized him and pinioned his arms.

"Better go with them," he growled when he had recovered his breath and Migishima pounded up to lend a hand. "Do what the lady says. Or she might hurt you."

Chapter XXIII

Even though Otani could easily have justified the use of his official car for the forty-mile journey to Kyoto, he and Hanae had decided to go by public transport. It was the first time Hanae had travelled on the new subway line which runs from Kyoto Station to the northern outskirts of the city, and she was duly impressed by its clean efficiency, contrasting it to her husband, as they emerged from Imadegawa Station into the open air opposite the grounds of the Old Imperial Palace, with the noisy, rattle-trap transport arrangements beneath the city of Osaka.

It was a dull afternoon but they were both in a good mood. Hanae was conscious of looking her best in a dull cream kimono with touches of pink; a little young for her but justified by the season of the year. Otani for his part had been in high spirits since he arrived home late the previous evening, full of the news that the man apprehended with Abdul Ghafoor Khan by the Migishimas outside the Kobe Mosque had turned out to be the First Secretary from the

167

Embassy of Pakistan. The police had had no option but to let him go as soon as he produced his diplomatic identity card, but the Pakistani Ambassador would have a lot of explaining to do when summoned to the Ministry of Foreign Affairs in Tokyo.

Otani's staff were under no such obligation in the case of Khan, with whom Otani himself had had two protracted and delicately managed conversations, one late on Friday afternoon after a long telephone conversation with Kimura and the second that very morning. It was a nuisance that Kimura was unwell and thought he ought to stay at home for a day or two, but Otani managed well enough with the help of Hara and Noguchi. In any case and although he was rather mysterious about what was actually wrong with him, Otani felt that the extraordinary information Kimura had been able to provide justified his taking a day off.

"It was clever of you to think of the shoes," Hanae said as they began to stroll the few hundred yards past the campus of Doshisha University itself to the main gate of the adjoining Women's University, a separate entity belonging to the same foundation.

"I should have thought of them right away," Otani replied modestly. "It was several days before it occurred to me that they would both have had to take off their shoes at the main entrance to the hotel and that both Fuhaid's and the woman's ought to be there in the cupboard still. If it had been a proper traditional inn they'd have had an old man to take care of guests' shoes, but in that sort of place people are supposed to fend for themselves."

Hara and his staff had made short work of establishing beyond any doubt that the pair of woman's shoes Otani had brought back from Arima were identical in size and pattern of wear to a pair of Sachiko Chiba's obtained by Inspector Sugawa from the wardrobe department at the Takarazuka Grand Theatre.

Suddenly Otani stopped short and plucked at Hanae's sleeve. "Good heavens! Do you see what I see?"

About fifty yards ahead of them a taxi had pulled in. The back door swung open as the driver operated his remote control mechanism and a leg extended itself gingerly, accompanied by an aluminium crutch. Then the rest of Kimura followed, going through a series of ungainly manoeuvres as he hauled himself into an upright position and fumbled in his pocket for money while a second passenger also clambered out of the cab, a young foreign woman with vivid red hair. By this time the Otanis had arrived on the scene, and they waited quietly as Kimura pocketed his change and then swung round. The dressing on his head was not particularly conspicuous, but the plaster on his cheek was much bigger. Even so it was not nearly large enough either to cover the bruising and discoloration on that side of his face or to disguise the look of sheer horror which spread over the undamaged areas. The young woman with him looked pale and drawn, and stood quietly to one side.

"Good afternoon, Mr Kimura," Hanae said brightly. "How nice to see you here! What *have* you been doing to yourself?" Otani nodded in greeting, but said nothing.

A sickly smile gradually replaced Kimura's previous expression. "Oh. Good afternoon, Mrs Otani. Good afternoon, er. . .may I introduce my friend Miss Shulamit Steiner?" His facial injuries made him speak with some difficulty.

They all stood about indecisively for a few moments, the foreign girl hesitating before observing the courtesies. She struck Hanae as wanting to be polite, but obviously in something of a hurry. "*Hajimemashite*. Pleased to meet you," she muttered conventionally in Japanese at last. "*Dozo yoroshiku o-negai itashimasu*. Please show your favour to me." Then she turned to Kimura and spoke to him in English. "Look, I really have to go to the business meeting before the party. It's probably started already. Mind if I go ahead? You can take your time." Without waiting for him to reply she smiled wanly at Hanae, excused herself in Japanese, then made off.

169

"I'm glad to see you're feeling better, Kimura-kun," Otani said courteously. "May I ask what happened?"

"Ah. Yes, I should have explained, Chief," Kimura began miserably. "The fact is, I fell down some stairs. Sprained my ankle badly and bruised my face. And had to have a couple of stitches in my head where I cut it."

Hanae's reaction was immediate. "Oh, you poor man! You must be feeling wretched! I do hope you're taking care of yourself properly." She broke off as she caught sight of the expression on her husband's face and then began again. "You must be going to the KISS party. We are, too. My sister teaches here and is connected with it. Come, we must go in and find somewhere for you to sit down."

Otani spoke at last. "Actually, I'd quite like a word with Inspector Kimura before we go in," he said. "I wonder if. . .?"

"Of course," Hanae said at once. "I'll go and see if I can find Michiko. I don't suppose she's involved with the business meeting Mr Kimura's friend mentioned." She smiled at Kimura who gazed after her sadly as she made her way in the direction indicated on a hand-lettered sign referring to the KISS reception. He felt rather like a drowning man watching a lifebelt float away out of reach.

"Bad luck, Kimura. You've got some painful-looking bruising there." There was sympathy in Otani's voice, but then he spoiled everything with his next words. "The young lady seems to have emerged from the encounter without a scratch, though." Kimura drooped from his crutch and suddenly Otani hadn't the heart to go on. "Sorry, Kimura-kun. I realise that wasn't very funny. Look, let's sit down for a minute on that wall over there. I must tell you what I got out of that fellow Khan, then I need your advice about how we might set about tidying this thing up."

Kimura hobbled over to the low wall and Otani followed, standing over him quietly as he lowered himself into a sitting position. "Before we get on to that, though, a question. Don't you think that girl ought to be under arrest, Kimura?"

Chapter XXIV

"This is getting ridiculous," Otani said in an undertone to Hanae as her sister Michiko ushered them into a large room which enthusiastic but inexpert hands had tried to endow with a festive appearance. A large but shabby folding screen covered in gold-coloured paper had been placed against one wall to provide a background, behind a small dais with a microphone on a stand in front of it, and on a low table to one side of the dais there was a flower arrangement in a shallow black bowl. Tacked to the wall above the screen was a long horizontal banner inscribed with both Japanese and English words. The English version read:

KINKI INTERNATIONAL STUDENTS SOCIETY
14TH REGULER FREINDSHIP MEETING
AND SOCIAL PARTY

and Michiko, who was wearing black woollen leg-warmers under a voluminous and shapeless cotton tunic held more or less together by an enormous leather belt, tut-tutted fussily as she scrutinised it. "Mistakes, mistakes!" she said in the manner of one being intolerably put upon. "They really must ask one of the foreign members to check the English. They've spelt 'regular' wrongly."

Both the Otanis ignored her. "What is?" Hanae enquired. "Look over there. In the far corner."

The middle of the room was dominated by an arrangement of tables pushed together to form an enormous single surface, which had been covered with overlapping sheets of white paper held in place with drawing-pins. Another flower arrangement had pride of place in the middle, while large metal platters of small sandwiches were interspersed with smaller ones, some laden with fried chicken drumsticks, others with pieces of toast spread with savoury fish spread and decorated with morsels of olive, and yet others with heaps of chicken and vegetable kebabs on bamboo skewers. All were covered with plastic cling-film.

Then there were two large bowls of oranges, bananas and grapes, one at each end, and stacks of plates alongside plentiful supplies of throwaway chopsticks in paper envelopes at each corner. Strategically placed at intervals round the perimeter were clumps of bottles of Sapporo beer and Fanta orange juice surrounded by arrays of plain tumblers; and peering over the whole at the Otanis with a look of incredulity on his large face was Officer Migishima encased in a smart blue suit with his wife Junko smiling politely at his side and a Japanese girl beside her.

"Why, it's Mr and Mrs Migishima! How odd that they should be here too."

Otani nodded as Michiko detached herself from them and bore down upon a bespectacled girl who was fiddling with the microphone, which emitted tentative howls and ringing thumps from time to time. "It certainly is. I'm beginning to wonder if there's anybody at all policing Hyogo Prefecture at the moment."

Migishima became visibly more bemused when Kimura lurched through the door on his aluminium crutch, his sound

172

foot encased in a smart Italian shoe and the injured one in an unlaced Nike brand canvas training shoe in a sporty shade of bright blue with acid yellow flashes; but Kimura appeared not to notice his assistant as he collapsed into one of the straight chairs which lined each wall except the one with the screen placed against it.

Otani now felt truly sorry for him. Confirmation awaited the questioning of Sachiko Chiba, but although there was no way in which she could have accompanied him to the Arima Grand View Hotel in the late morning and left in his company after lunch, Otani was no longer in the slightest doubt that she had been the woman with Fuhaid in the afternoon.

The American girl, whom Otani had at once recognised as the woman he had seen at the Takarazuka Grand Theatre, had admitted having gone to Arima with Fuhaid in the morning, disguised in a black wig and dark glasses. During his first and secret absence from the hotel and after he had killed Abdalla, Fuhaid had provided her with an alibi by making a withdrawal using her Dai-ichi Bank cashcard and giving her the receipt.

The question of the shoes still nagged at Otani, and he meant to have the shoe-shops in Arima checked. There couldn't be many, and even in a hot-spring resort someone would be bound to remember a well-dressed woman customer turning up in backless indoor slippers; for unless his hypothesis was much mistaken, Sachiko Chiba could not have foreseen when she entered the hotel that she would have to abandon the shoes she deposited at the entrance. He had decided firmly to suppress any private reservations he had about Kimura's actions over the past few days, but had made it clear to him that Shulamit Steiner was to be placed under arrest immediately they were back in Hyogo Prefecture.

Although people were continually arriving there were still only about twenty people in the big room. The special business meeting involving the actual members of KISS which was being held in another room was evidently dragging on. Otani was on the point of going over to speak to the

Migishimas, whose presence intrigued him when Hanae's sister, who had bustled out after berating the hapless girl by the microphone, reappeared in the doorway nodding and smiling as though modestly accepting praise for some outstanding achievement.

Hard upon her heels was a flock of KISS members. The young Japanese men and women for the most part looked both earnest and troubled. The Europeans seemed to be either bored or amused, but most of them brightened perceptibly at the sight of the food and some headed for the table, then hesitated when they saw the cling-film defences still in place. The older hands among them waited philosophically, having learned through experience of the iron Japanese rule that speeches must be endured and a toast proposed before they would be allowed to eat.

Otani had no idea what the distinguishing marks of either Jews or Moslems might be, but as the remainder of the members entered the room and arranged themselves in little clumps here and there he was struck by the characteristics of two very close-knit groups. One consisted of eight or nine men with skin colouring of various shades but generally reminiscent of Abdul Ghafoor Khan's. The other comprised six men, three of them bearded though youthful and wearing odd little blue and white skullcaps pinned to the backs of their heads, and two women, one of them Shulamit Steiner who looked around for Kimura and then went and sat beside him. The members of the first group looked out of sorts, even belligerent, while those in the second were flushed and seemed rather pleased with themselves.

The girl in charge of the microphone now spoke into it briefly in what sounded to Otani vaguely like English, and then bowed to Michiko, who took some typewritten sheets out of her bag and addressed the assembly at much greater length in the same language, stumbling here and there over her script but also pausing from time to time to emphasise a point with an arch smile. Otani was beginning to hope that she must surely soon come to an end when she said something

174

which clearly offended the bellicose contingent and gratified Shulamit and her friends who clapped and cheered loudly over the noisy objections of the opposition.

Michiko faltered and stopped, whereupon one of the angry ones shouted something which was followed by an audible intake of breath from almost all the other foreigners. The irate Moslems then turned their backs ostentatiously on Michiko and made as if to march out of the room in a body but were physically prevented from doing so by a phalanx of apparently outraged young male foreigners including the bearded youths, and Otani belatedly realised that a melee was developing.

He tried to catch Migishima's eye to warn him to keep out of it but he was too late. He was already in the thick of it with Junko at his side, bellowing "I am a police officer," and fielding blows from both camps impartially. Junko for her part had a firm hold on one of the Moslems who seemed to have gone almost berserk with outrage; possibly, Otani thought as he headed quickly towards the microphone, because his captor was a woman. Michiko looked as if she was about to faint but he brushed her aside peremptorily.

"STOP!" It was one of the few English words Otani knew, and he shouted it into the microphone only once, but it had a remarkable effect, and the fighting began to subside. He continued in Japanese. "Inspector Kimura! Will you please explain in English that there are four police officers in this room and that this disturbance must cease at once."

Until the fighting began there had been no real need for a microphone at all, and Kimura's voice could be heard quite clearly all over the room as he repeated Otani's message. Otani was in the meantime pushing his way over to Kimura and when he arrived whispered urgently to him. "Just calm them down, for heaven's sake, and let's get out of here. We're totally out of order in intervening in this at all. Let those who want to leave do so. Take their names, I suppose, but I shall have enough apologising to do as it is when the Kyoto force get to hear about all this." He then turned to the Migishimas,

175

each of whom was still grasping a struggling young man. "Let them go," he hissed as Kimura resumed his harangue, and was astounded when Migishima firmly shook his head.

"We want these men for questioning, sir," he said. "In connection with the death of Dr Ahmed el Abdalla. They're the other ones we were looking for at the mosque yesterday."

Chapter XXV

"I've missed you," Hanae said simply as they left the house after lunch on the following Saturday. Otani had returned from three days and two nights in Tokyo late on the previous evening and had been too tired to do much more than take a bath and go to bed. He had however reassured her that he had eaten a meal on the train and, with a slight smile, told her that Kimura had telephoned him on board the train to report that no untoward incidents had been observed by the uniformed man on duty outside the Kobe Mosque that day and that he, Kimura, would be duty officer on Saturday. "With or without his crutches, he didn't say," Otani had added, "but I intend to take the day off."

He had slept till after nine, then spent the balmy, sunny morning sitting on the back porch with the newspaper, occasionally contemplating their tiny formal garden and once fetching his special secateurs to trim some of the needles of a gnarled pine tree no more than a foot high in its bowl, one of the bonsai he had inherited from his father.

Hanae had left him to his own devices and quite expected him to drift through the remainder of the day in much the same way, but while they were eating their lunch of fried noodles he had suddenly announced that he felt like going for a stroll and invited Hanae to join him. "We might go to the zoo," he had suggested. It seemed an odd idea to her, but it was a beautiful day, and she felt in vaguely holiday mood as Otani slid the wooden gate closed behind them and they headed towards the main road which would lead them down the hill.

"I'm glad to be home, too. I hate having to sit round a table at the National Police Agency undergoing an inquisition. At least they weren't hinting this time that we handled everything wrongly. There was a fellow from the Foreign Ministry there who was quite complimentary. Ambassador Atsugi must have been in touch with them over the details. Oh, and somebody from the Ministry of Justice. A rather formidable young woman. I was astonished – she didn't seem in the least intimidated by the rest of us."

"Quite right, too. Wait till Mrs Migishima becomes an inspector."

Otani laughed. "She's quite lively enough as it is. I don't know about promotion. We'll think about it if she can persuade that husband of hers to stop arresting everybody in sight, perhaps."

"You managed to clear everything up, then?"

Otani took a deep breath of the soft spring air and looked around appreciatively at the familiar street. They were passing the liquor shop on the corner. "I don't know that one could ever say that about any case, especially a messy one like this has been. We must pick up some sake on the way home. When I was in the kitchen this morning I noticed the bottle was nearly empty. Yes, well, I suppose we achieved all we could. What with the information we teased out of the Pakistani fellow and what the Jewish girl and Sachiko Chiba volunteered, the picture began to shape itself. Shall we walk to the zoo, or do you want to get a bus?"

"Oh, let's walk," Hanae said. "I want to hear all about it. It's tantalising to have heard bits and pieces and not to know how they fit together."

"There are always bits left over, Ha-chan. We haven't finished with either of those two young ladies yet, although I'm quite sure neither of them killed the Arab – I mean the Jew. It's an extraordinary story, and I shall never get it sorted out in my own mind. Maybe Hara will be able to make head or tail of it. Mind if I have a cigarette?"

Hanae had applauded and encouraged his efforts to give up smoking, but had never nagged him about it, and was surprised that he asked. "No, of course not." They stopped while Otani lit up, and he took up the tale again as they moved on.

"The long and the short of it is that both the men who died were agents. The Foreign Ministry people in their own devious ways have established that the man who called himself Fuhaid was an Israeli under what they call deep cover. He'd got himself fixed up with a United Arab Emirates passport, and was fluent in Arabic. He'd been sent here to infiltrate the mosque, which he did very successfully, to find out about links between the Arabs resident in Japan and our own terrorist people. You remember. A group of them attacked the airport in Tel Aviv in 1972 with grenades and killed a lot of people. It seems the Israeli secret service has a long memory and a habit of exacting vengeance. He completely fooled everybody associated with the mosque, including the Pakistani who became quite a crony of his. But he didn't fool everybody else, obviously. Questions must have been asked about him outside Japan, possibly even as a result of information unknowingly passed on by the Pakistani to his fanatical friends in the Muslim Brotherhood – Hara seems to have guessed right about that."

Otani fell silent for a while and they walked some distance while Hanae waited patiently for him to go on. "Meantime Fuhaid had succumbed to temptation. He'd had an affair with Sachiko Chiba while she was in Israel, and knew of course

179

that she was living in the area. He sought her out and they soon took up with each other again. By the time Fuhaid realised that Abdalla was close to uncovering him she was hopelessly in love with him, and when he decided he had to kill Abdalla she willingly conspired to give him an alibi while he did it. She had an additional reason – Abdalla had been spying on Fuhaid and learned of her relationship with him. It was Abdalla who was trying to blackmail her into telling him what she knew about Fuhaid. He never knew that the letters he wrote to her went straight to the Takarazuka police, who had of course had to talk to her about them. Are you still with me?"

Hanae nodded. "I *think* so," she said uncertainly.

"Good. Well, Fuhaid must have been a persuasive fellow. He managed to convince his Pakistani friend not only that Abdalla was an agent – which of course he was – but also that he was on the other side and had to be done away with in some way which had a fair chance of not arousing suspicion. Hence the hit-and-run murder with the taxi, which was all fixed up. At least Fuhaid did his own dirty work, but then at the last minute Sachiko Chiba's rehearsal and performance schedule had been changed, and she couldn't go to Arima with him in the morning. But of course some months ago this American girlfriend of Kimura's had turned up. She too had met Fuhaid in Israel – he was in a photograph Kimura saw by chance in her flat – and, being a close friend of Sachiko Chiba, had to be let into the secret before long, even though so far as we know only Chiba-san was his mistress."

"So the American girl substituted for Chiba-san in the morning? She's very beautiful, don't you think?"

"What? Oh, yes, I suppose she is in a way. She has a Japanese grandfather or grandmother, according to Kimura. Anyway, you guessed right. She volunteered to be there all day, but Fuhaid insisted on the change-over in the afternoon. Hence the disguise, though with that red hair of hers she'd probably have used one anyway. It's my belief that Fuhaid always intended to commit suicide after he had successfully

180

removed Abdalla: his cover was getting very thin with both women knowing who he really was. But he wanted to be with the one he loved at the end. So he took Miss Steiner out of the hotel, mailed his suicide note to Khan, and came back with Chiba-san. Made love to her for the last time, then took a bath and cut his wrists in it. The colour of the water concealed what he had done from her until it was too late. All she could do was slip out of the hotel and hope she would never be traced."

"Poor, poor woman. What a ghastly thing to happen." Hanae's imagination was seized with the horror of the scene, and although the sunshine was very warm she felt physically chilled.

"At least she knows she was greatly loved," Otani said quietly, and then fell silent until they were in sight of the gateway to the Nada Zoo.

A few moments later he stopped short and seized Hanae's arm. "Come in here a minute," he said urgently, and led her under the awning of a bookshop which displayed many of its wares on moveable stands on the pavement. "Look. No, over there." Hanae peered in the direction he was indicating.

"It can't be. . ."

"It is. It's Ninja Noguchi."

Hanae was intrigued. Even at a distance of more than a hundred metres there could be no mistaking the familiar figure heading for the zoo entrance. "But who are those people with him?"

Hanae watched as a peculiar smile spread over her husband's face and broadened into one of his very rare grins. "Well, the tall one in the yellow sports shirt is Inspector Hara. The pregnant lady must be his wife, and the little girl holding Ninja's hand and dragging him along must be their daughter. I never expected to live to see the day. . .come on, let's go and talk to them."

Hanae held back. "No, please not. Even from the back he looks so contented. I wouldn't want to . . . embarrass Mr Noguchi. Please, darling."

Otani looked at her, the quality of his smile now quite different. "All right. I think I understand. Let's go and find a cup of coffee and a cake instead, shall we?"

Hanae gave just one backward glance at the little group at the zoo gates as they strolled away in the direction from which they had come. Hara and Noguchi seemed to be arguing over who should pay, with the little girl dancing excitedly beside them.

"Thank you, I'd like a cup of coffee," she said composedly. "Oh, by the way, there's still one thing I'd like to know – about the Moslems, I mean."

Otani thought he detected a note of slight embarrassment in her voice, and looked at her in some surprise. "Oh, what's that?"

Hanae coughed, hesitated and then avoided his eye. "Do you think you could find out from Mr Kimura what it was that young man in Kyoto shouted at Michiko? I mean, it would be so interesting to know."

Otani nodded gravely. "Yes, it would, wouldn't it? I'll ask him on Monday."